FRIIIGHT NIGHT

GOOSEBUMPS®

Also available as ebooks

ALSO AVAILABLE:

FRIIIGHT NIGHT

R.L. STINE

SCHOLASTIC INC.

Goosebumps book series created by Parachute Press, Inc.
Copyright © 2023 by Scholastic Inc.

All rights reserved. Published by Scholastic Inc., *Publishers since 1920.* SCHOLASTIC, GOOSEBUMPS, GOOSEBUMPS HORRORLAND, and associated logos are trademarks and/or registered trademarks of Scholastic Inc.

ISBN 978-1-338-75223-6

10 9 8 7 6 5 4 3 2 1   23 24 25 26 27

Printed in the U.S.A.   40
First printing 2023

SLAPPY HERE, EVERYONE.

Welcome to My World.

Yes, it's *SlappyWorld*—you're only *screaming* in it! Hahaha.

Now that I've said hello, please go away.

No. I mean it. Stop reading. Don't go any farther.

I'm writing in my private journal, and I don't like anyone looking over my shoulder to see what I'm saying about myself.

When I write in my journal, I'm always very honest. I tell myself honestly how I am the greatest. I write about how wonderful I am. And how smart I am.

I'm so smart, I can spell my name with my eyes closed. Seriously.

I'm so amazing, sometimes it's hard to find words to describe myself. Words fail me, and I end up making *kissing* sounds to myself.

Awesome just doesn't say it. *Terrific* is kind of weak. *Spectacular* doesn't quite do it.

Adoring myself is a special time for me. A private time between me and myself.

So, beat it. Get lost. Stop reading this. Take a hint—go away.

Okay, okay. Tell you what. I'll give you a story to read while I enjoy my private moment.

Some of this story takes place in a school basement. You're probably afraid to go down to the basement of your school, aren't you? That's because you know a monster's living there behind the furnace.

Well, a boy named Kelly Crosby is about to find out about his school monster—close-up! I call the story *Friiight Night*.

You'll see why.

I'll let Kelly tell the story . . .

Let's say you were an ant, and you lived with your ant family in a little dirt hole under someone's porch. Then one day, someone dug up the dirt hole and carried it in a truck a few hundred miles and dropped it in the middle of the world's biggest ant farm.

How would you feel?

Well, you probably can't answer that question—unless you're an ant. I'm trying to describe how I feel, having moved from Little Hills Village, New Hampshire, to Great Newton, Massachusetts. I don't mean that Little Hills Village is a dirt hole. It's just tiny compared to Great Newton, see.

I'm Kelly Crosby. I'm twelve. And you can probably tell that I'm a little messed up by my family's move. In the middle of the school year. To a town where I don't have a single friend or even know anyone.

I was in the back seat of our car, on my way to my first day of school, and I started to text my friend Charlene Morse back home. But I decided I had too much to say, so I called her instead.

"Charlene, if I was an ant, I'd say, 'Someone, please step on me!'" I groaned.

She was silent for a moment. Then she said, "I hate ants. Why are you talking about ants?"

"Because I feel like one," I said. "And because there were ants in the kitchen when we moved in. Mom put down so many ant traps, you can't walk barefoot in there."

"Well, stop talking about them," she said. "What's new?"

"Huh? What's new? *Everything* is new," I replied.

"Kelly, you don't sound happy," Charlene said.

"Is an ant happy in the ocean?" I exclaimed.

She sighed. "Kelly, I'm going to hang up now. If you say the word *ant* one more time . . ."

"We have mosquitoes, too," I said. "I-I guess I miss Little Hills Village. Tell me what's up. What's going on there?"

"You know what's going on here," she replied. "Nothing. It's so boring here—"

"I like boring," I said.

"Okay, Kelly. I'll tell you the big news. Two dogs got into a dogfight on the lower school playground last Friday. That's the big news."

"Who won?" I asked.

We both laughed.

I think Charlene and I are good friends because we have the same sense of humor. We make the same jokes, and we both laugh at the same things.

But then she turned serious. "Listen to me. You're so lucky. You'll love Adams Prep. A big school will be so much more exciting."

"Who likes exciting?" I said.

"Stop it," she snapped. "I'm totally jealous of you, Kelly. New kids. A big new school. Just think. You can be a new person with a new personality."

"Huh?" I replied. "What's wrong with my old personality?"

"I didn't know you *had* one!" she joked.

Or maybe it was a joke.

"Did you buy new clothes for the new school?" Charlene asked. "Did you throw away that *Puppy Pals* T-shirt?"

"You're not funny," I said. "You know I wore that shirt ironically."

"I hope you burned that other shirt you thought was such a riot."

"Which one?" I asked. "The one that said *Don't Read This Shirt*? Everyone laughed at that T-shirt."

"Those were sympathy laughs," Charlene said. "Let's be honest. You were kind of a wimp here. Now you have a chance to try a bold new personality. How lucky to be able to start over!"

Mom pulled the car to the curb. I gazed out at the tall, redbrick Adams Prep school building. Groups of kids were hurrying to the wide front entrance.

The school was huge.

"Gotta go," I told Charlene. "We're here."

"Good luck," she said.

"Does an ant need good luck in a forest?" I said.

Mom turned around and squinted at me. "Stop talking about ants."

2

A big guy bumped me from behind as I stepped into the front hall. I guess I was moving too slowly. The noise of lockers slamming and kids shouting and laughing rang against the tile walls. There were more kids in the front hall than I had ever seen in my entire school.

Two guys were playing keep-away, tossing another guy's backpack across the hall. Two girls in red-and-blue cheerleader outfits were practicing a cheer at the top of their lungs.

A tall kid in blue shades with a blue cap tilted over his face leaned against a locker, playing a small silver harmonica.

A girl sailed into the hall on a skateboard. Kids dodged out of her way.

"This is a fun place," I muttered to myself. *I'm going to like it here. I'll get used to it, and I'll start to love it.*

But I already had a problem. I didn't know how to find my classroom.

My school in Little Hills Village was a low, flat building. It didn't take long to walk from one end to the other.

But the halls at Adams Prep were at least half a mile long. The building was three floors, not one. I saw an elevator at the back wall. A sign next to it read: TEACHERS AND STAFF ONLY.

I shifted the backpack on my shoulders. It was mostly empty. I hadn't received any textbooks or anything yet. I ducked as a red Frisbee flew over my head.

I turned to the kid who threw it. "Ms. Waxman's class?" I asked.

"Downstairs."

"But where are the stairs?"

He didn't hear me. He had chased after his friend, the other Frisbee player.

Kelly, you can find the stairs, I told myself.

Sure, I felt a little overwhelmed by the crowd of kids and the noise. I get overwhelmed sometimes. Mom says I'm *sensitive.* I think that's her polite way of saying I'm a wimp.

But I'm not helpless. And just because I was used to a tiny village and a tiny school didn't mean I couldn't handle something new.

Charlene's words rang in my ears: "Now you have a chance to try a bold new personality."

So I gritted my teeth, pushed my shoulders forward, and made my way through the crowd. The hall branched off into two long corridors, and I took the one on the left. I passed the principal's office. Through the office window, I saw a mob of kids and teachers lined up at the front desk.

I passed some classrooms. Then I stopped at a red-painted wooden door. I pulled it open and saw a metal stairway that led down.

"That wasn't so hard, Kelly," I scolded myself.

I stepped into a dimly lit stairwell. The air felt warm and it smelled like a basement, kind of musty and sour. I listened for a moment. Silence.

I hesitated. Why wasn't anyone else on the stairs? Then I let go of the door and started down.

I was halfway to the bottom when I heard a deep growl.

I stopped. And listened. Was it an animal growl?

Yes. I heard another one, low and angry. A dog?

Another rumbling growl sent a chill down my back. I turned, grabbed the banister, and pulled myself back up the stairs.

I stepped into the hall and shut the red door behind me.

What had I heard? What kind of animal was down there?

Why was there some kind of animal in the basement of this school?

I leaned against the door and waited for my heart to stop pounding. Everyone was hurrying to their class-rooms. A buzzer went off above my head. I jumped about a mile. I guessed that was the morning bell.

I saw a kid across the hall pulling books from an open locker. "Hey," I called to him, and headed over.

He had curly copper-colored hair and a face full of freckles. He closed his locker door and turned to me. "What's up?"

"I-I'm just starting today," I stammered. "Do you know where Ms. Waxman's classroom is?"

He swung his backpack over his shoulders. "I'm in Waxman's class," he said. "Follow me."

"Awesome," I said. "I'm new. I . . . got kinda lost."

He snickered. "I've been here for three years, and I still get turned around." He studied me for a moment. "Where you from?"

"Little Hills Village."

He snickered again. "Is that a real place? It sounds made up."

"It's very tiny," I said. "You can find it on Google Maps, but you have to really zoom in to see it."

That made him laugh. His blue eyes flashed. He had a friendly laugh.

"I'm Gordon Willey," he said. "A lot of kids call me Gordo, and I hate it."

"Okay, Gordo," I said. I couldn't resist. It made him laugh again. I told him my name.

I thought maybe we could be friends.

The hall was emptying out. A second buzzer rang, echoing down the long corridor. I followed him up a wide stairway.

"I can help you find things," he said. "Like, there's no boys' room on the first floor. You have to hold it in till you get to the second floor."

"Good to know," I said.

"And the lunchroom is on three," he said. "Weird, huh?"

He stopped at a room marked 104-B. "Here you go," he said. "Waxman's room. You'll like her. She's seriously nice."

"Awesome," I said. "Some kid told me Ms. Waxman's classroom was downstairs."

"They were playing a joke on you. There aren't any classes down there. It's just the basement."

I started to thank him, but he interrupted me. "Hey, you got here just in time for Friiight Night. Good luck, Kelly."

"Huh?" I wasn't sure I heard him right. "Friiight Night? What's that? Why do I need good luck?"

But he was already in the room, and I didn't get an answer.

Ms. Waxman was standing with two girls behind her desk. They were looking at something on an iPhone. "That's rad," she said to the girls. "Don't tell your parents I said so."

She turned as I walked in. "The new kid!" she exclaimed.

I nodded and took a few steps toward her.

"Know how I figured that out?" she asked. "Because I've never seen you before."

I laughed. She was making a joke. "You're a good detective," I said.

She was young, with straight black hair cut very short, dark eyes, and a nice smile. I saw a tattoo of a red heart on her wrist. Teachers at my old school wouldn't dare have tattoos.

She blew a metal whistle and everyone got quiet. "I used to be a soccer coach," she explained. "And I just can't bear to give up my whistle."

She's funny, I thought. *I think I'm going to like her.*

Ms. Waxman leaned over her desk and raised a sheet of paper. "You're Kelly Crosby," she said. "Hey,

11

everyone, this is Kelly Crosby," she announced. "Where are you from, Kelly?"

"Little Hills Village," I said.

She nodded. "Oh yes. I drove through there once. But I sneezed and I missed it."

A few kids laughed.

"It's very small," I said. "And my school was small, too."

"I'll bet it was so small, your shadow had to wait outside!" She grinned, enjoying the kids' laughter.

I never had a comedian for a teacher before, I thought.

"Well, let's all welcome Kelly to Adams Prep," she said. "And be nice to him. He probably finds you all pretty scary. I know *I* find you scary!"

I could feel my face turning red. The kids were all staring at me, studying me, I guess. It was too much attention, and I'm an easy blusher.

Ms. Waxman pointed to a chair-desk combo by the window near the back of the room. "There's an empty desk, Kelly," she said. "Why don't you take it?"

I nodded and started for the desk.

"You have a lot of catching up to do," she called after me. "Especially with Friiight Night coming so soon."

I slid into the chair and dropped my backpack to the floor. "What is Friiight Night?" I asked.

But she had turned to talk to a girl in the front row and didn't hear me.

I gazed around the room, searching for Gordon. He was near the back against the other wall. He had his head down, concentrating on something in a blue notebook.

Ms. Waxman perched on the edge of her desk. "I'm going to pass out a Tournament Quiz in a moment," she said. "Or should I just pass out?"

She waited for the laugh.

Then she continued. "First, I have an announcement to make. Our class has been named Activities Committee for Friiight Night."

A few kids gasped. A few cried out in surprise. I couldn't tell if it was good news or bad.

"You know what that means," the teacher continued. "We have to think of some fun activities and entertainment for everyone." She gazed around the class. "I can see you're already thinking. Well ... that's your homework assignment. Make a list of five things that would be good for Friiight Night."

I raised my hand. I *had* to find out what Friiight Night was. How could I do the homework assignment if I didn't know what it was?

But Ms. Waxman didn't see me. She had turned away again and picked up a stack of papers from her desk. Then she began walking through the rows of desks, handing them out.

She stopped at my desk. "Listen, Kelly," she said, "I know you're new. But you have to try your very best on the Tournament Quizzes."

"Seriously—?" I started.

Her eyes narrowed and her smile faded. "There will be five more quizzes, and you have to do well. You don't want to come in last in the class," she said. "You don't want to be the monster's date on Friiight Night."

Huh? The monster's date?

"Friiight Night? What's Friiight Night?" I demanded.

She set the paper down on my desk. "Start the quiz," she said. "You're going to need as much time as possible."

"But—"

"You can ask one of the kids to tell you about Friiight Night later," she said. "Good luck."

Why was everyone wishing me good luck today?

5

Saturday, I did a FaceTime call with Charlene back home. "Do you miss me?" I asked.

"Not really," she said.

I think she was joking. I told you, we have the same sense of humor.

"I have a lot of new friends who are cooler than you," she said.

"Name six," I replied.

She laughed.

"I have kind of a new friend," I said. "His name is Gordon. But it's hard to make friends when you come in the middle of the year. Everyone already knows everyone."

"I don't feel sorry for you, Kelly," Charlene said. "It's so boring here. I keep wishing for those two dogs to have another fight on the playground."

"I made a plan to go bowling with Gordon next Saturday," I said.

"Huh? You? Bowling? Will you have someone help you lift the bowling ball?"

"Haha," I said. "I always wanted to try it. Which

15

was impossible since there's no bowling alley in Little Hills Village."

"Tell me about it."

"I passed a really cool one a few blocks from school," I said. "It had this huge neon sign with three bowling balls flying in the air."

"Too much excitement," Charlene said. Sometimes she can be seriously sarcastic.

I had my phone facing me, propped against my laptop. I sat in my desk chair and juggled three balls while I talked to Charlene. My uncle Pete was a circus clown, and he taught me how to juggle when I was five.

"Are you showing off your one talent again?" Charlene asked.

"You're jealous," I said. I began juggling the balls faster.

"I'm jealous because you're in a big, new school," she said. "And I have Mr. Potner for the second year in a row."

"Potner rules," I said.

Then I decided to change the subject and tell her what I had really called about. "The school has this thing coming up real soon. It's called Friiight Night. With three I's."

"Maybe you need three eyes to go to it," Charlene said. "What is it? Some kind of party?"

"I guess," I said. "But I can't get anyone to tell me what it is. I just know it's a big deal. They keep talking about it. And every time I ask what it is, they say they'll tell me about it later, but then they don't."

"Maybe it's like a Halloween party," Charlene suggested. "Everyone dresses up and tries to be scary."

"Maybe," I said. "The teacher said there's a monster. Maybe that's what she meant."

Talking to Charlene was already making me feel better. I was wondering what that monster thing was all about. It was probably a scary party with scary costumes. That made sense.

I tossed one of the balls too high, missed it, and it bounced onto the floor. I picked it up and started juggling again, more carefully.

"My class is in charge of activities," I told Charlene. "We're supposed to think some up. But how can I when I don't really know what Friiight Night is?"

"Maybe you could give juggling lessons," she replied. "That could be fun."

"I don't know," I said. "I guess—"

I stopped because I heard a knock on the front door. I jumped up and crossed to my bedroom window. Gazing down at our front stoop, I saw Gordon and two other kids.

"Talk later," I told Charlene. "Gotta go."

I ended the call and tucked the phone into my jeans pocket. Then I hurried to the front door. I pulled it open to see Gordon with a girl and another boy behind him. Gordon lived around the corner. I'd seen him riding his bike down my street. All three of them were in my class.

"Hey, what's up?" I said.

17

"Come with us, Kelly," Gordon said. He grabbed my arm and started to pull me from the doorway.

"What? Where are we going?" I demanded.

"You've been in school a week," he said. "It's time for you to meet the monster."

I closed the door behind me, and we started to walk toward school. It was late afternoon and warm and sunny. Someone in the neighborhood was having a barbecue. A gust of smoke carried the aroma of hamburgers.

No one spoke. They were walking quickly, taking long strides, and I had to hurry to catch up. "Gordon." I tapped his shoulder. "It's Saturday. Isn't the school closed on Saturday?"

"No worries," he said. "You need to come with us today."

"Is this some kind of Adams Prep tradition?" I asked.

He shook his head. "It's not a tradition," he answered. "It's a school *rule*."

"You meet the monster after your first week of school," the girl said. Her name was Penny May. She was nice. She had helped me find the art room last week when I was walking around in circles.

She stepped up beside me as we crossed to the next block. "Kelly, are you scared?"

"Huh?" I squinted at her. "Should I be scared?" I suddenly remembered the growls in the basement. "Seriously. Should I be scared?"

No one answered. I felt a chill at the back of my neck.

Gordon waved to an SUV that slowly rolled past, filled with kids I recognized from school. "Just remember, Kelly, don't show any fear."

"Don't shake or whimper or anything," Penny May said.

I choked a little. "Now you're starting to scare me."

Gordon stopped walking and turned to me. "No worries. Adams has the best school monster in the state."

"Yeah," Kwame, the boy behind me, spoke up. "Those snobs at Madison Academy are always bragging about their monster," he said. "But Skwerm rules!"

I stared at him. "Skwerm?"

"What's a Skwerm?" I demanded.

"You'll see," Kwame said.

I followed them into the school through one of the side entrances. The hall must have just been washed. It smelled of strong detergent.

There was no one around. Our shoes thudded loudly in the empty hall as we made our way toward the back. Gordon stopped at the red door that led to the basement.

"Hey, wait. Someone tell me what we're doing," I said.

No one answered me.

"Skwerm totally slaps!" Gordon said. "He can beat Burrrph any day of the week."

"I bet Skwerm can beat Burrrph with his claws tied behind his back," Penny May added.

"Skwerm could *eat* Burrrph!" Kwame exclaimed. "Wouldn't that be awesome?"

The three of them burst out laughing.

I watched them, thinking hard. Then I *finally* figured out what was going on.

"I get it," I said. "Oh, wow. I finally get it."

They stared at me.

"This is a joke you play on all the new kids," I said. "Okay. Okay. You really had me going for a while. But now I get it."

Gordon shook his head and frowned at me. "Joke? What makes you think it's a joke?"

"We don't joke about Skwerm," Kwame said.

Gordon pulled open the red door.

I gulped loudly when I heard the angry animal growl floating up from the bottom of the stairs. I felt another chill at the back of my neck. "Uh . . . guys . . . what *is* that?" I uttered.

Gordon held the door open and gave me a push into the stairwell. "Let's go, Kelly. Down the stairs. I hope Skwerm likes you."

SLAPPY HERE, EVERYONE.

So Kelly is about to meet Skwerm. Think they'll become best friends?

I don't think so.

Meanwhile, back in Little Hills Village, Kelly's friend Charlene is worried about him.

Guess what, folks? She has *good reason* to be worried! Hahaha!

SLAPPY BECK EVERYONE

"Hello. Mrs. Crosby? This is Charlene. From Little Hills Village."

"Oh, hi, Charlene. How are things back home?"

"The same. Exactly the same."

"Are you trying to reach Kelly? He isn't here."

"I know. Do you know where he is? I've been texting him for an hour, and he hasn't answered."

"A bunch of kids came by and took him to school, Charlene."

"But he always answers my texts. I tried calling him, too. And it went right to voice mail."

"I haven't heard from him, either. I guess there's something special going on at school since it's Saturday. Is there a reason you wanted to reach him?"

"Haha. I wanted to tell him the big excitement. There was *another* dogfight on the lower school playground. Second one in two weeks!"

"Whoa. That *is* exciting, Charlene. Probably made the Little Hills newspaper! Ha. Kelly will like that story."

"If I ever reach him."

"Well, I'll tell Kelly to text you when he gets home."

"I hope he's okay. It's so weird that he hasn't answered."

"Don't you worry," Mrs. Crosby said. "I'm sure he's just fine."

Gordon had his hands on my back and kept me moving down the stairs. Behind me, Penny May and Kwame jammed the stairwell so that I couldn't turn around and escape.

The air grew hot and damp and smelled like stale sweat. I took one step at a time. My legs felt rubbery, and I realized my heart was beating at a fast rhythm, like a drum machine.

Down below, I could hear some kind of creature breathing noisily, with heavy grunts and deep-throated snarls.

I stopped two-thirds of the way down. "This isn't a joke?" My voice came out high and shrill.

"Keep going," Gordon said. "You don't want to keep Skwerm waiting. He isn't the most patient school monster in the state."

"Maybe some other time," I said. "I promised my dad I'd rake the leaves today."

"It's spring, Kelly," Kwame said. "There won't be any leaves on the ground for five or six months."

"I can wait," I said.

Down below, the creature bellowed loudly. The roar made the stairwell walls buzz. The banister shook in my hand. Or was that my hand shaking?

I stepped onto the concrete basement floor. The air was chokingly hot. Drops of sweat ran down my cheeks.

I stared at the enormous black boiler that filled the room, the boiler that heated the entire school. Pipes rose up from it in every direction, like tree branches.

Gordon, Penny May, and Kwame huddled behind me. "Wait here for Skwerm," Gordon whispered in my ear. "Stop shaking."

"I-I don't think I can," I stammered. "Maybe I could just FaceTime him."

The floor shook beneath us. A shadow stretched across the floor. I heard a wet, squishing sound. Noisy breathing. The shadow grew wider.

And then, with a loud rumble, the monster lumbered out from behind the boiler.

I let out a scream. I couldn't hold it in.

The monster's four round red eyes blinked at the sound. Four eyes!

He was huge! I think he was as big as a rhinoceros. I've never seen a rhinoceros, but I'm pretty sure he was as big as one.

The creature had wrinkled, leathery skin like a rhinoceros, too. His head bobbed on enormous shoulders. It looked like a gorilla head covered in blue bumps. Dozens of blue bumps. Were they warts?

The blue warts circled his enormous eyes and covered his short snout. His thick lips hung open, revealing rows of jagged yellow teeth.

I stared open-mouthed, trying to believe what I was seeing. His shoulders slid up and down as he pulled himself forward, grunting with each step.

And what were those things poking up from his shoulders? Were they mushrooms? Yes. Mushrooms growing on his shoulders.

Gordon had moved behind me. Was he using me as a shield?

He put his hands on my back. "Stop shaking," he whispered again. "I'm warning you. Don't let Skwerm see your fear."

"T-too late!" I stuttered.

10

The creature's red eyes locked onto mine. The big gorilla nostrils flared in and out. He grunted with every breath. But as our staring contest continued, the grunting turned to a low, steady rumble.

Like a dog warning that it's about to attack.

He didn't blink. Only his chest moved as his breathing grew even noisier. The mushrooms on his shoulders trembled. His mouth opened suddenly, in a loud hiccup.

I gasped.

Gordon could see this wasn't going well. He stepped beside me. "Skwerm, this is our new friend Kelly," he said. "Kelly is a new student. Kelly, I want you to meet Skwerm, the best school monster in the world."

I nodded. "Uh . . . hi," I choked out.

What was I supposed to do? Shake hands with him?

Did he have hands? If he did, they were hidden behind his back.

Gordon gave me a shove. "Quick—tell him how awesome he is."

I opened my mouth to speak. But I choked on my own tongue. "Uh . . . uh . . . uh . . ." I couldn't get any words out. I was shaking too hard for my brain to work.

Suddenly, Skwerm tossed back his big gorilla head. His red eyes bulged. He opened his jaws and let out a furious roar.

"Oh nooo." I sank back as the monster rumbled forward, taking heavy, squishing footsteps toward me.

"Oh, wow," Gordon muttered. He and the other two kids had already leaped back onto the stairs. "Oh, wow. I don't think he likes you."

I froze. My breath caught in my throat.

The monster's shadow washed over me as it attacked.

Somehow ... somehow ... I forced myself to spin away from it. I ducked my head and lowered my shoulder. And like a running back, I darted forward. I shoved Gordon, Kwame, and Penny May out of my way. And I thundered up the stairs.

I heard their surprised cries behind me. And I heard another deafening, angry roar from the monster.

I stumbled near the top. Got my balance. Kept running. Not even breathing. Not thinking. Just moving my feet.

I reached the hall and kept going. I didn't stop until I was outside. On the grass at the side of the school, I lowered my hands to my knees and struggled to catch my breath.

My head was spinning. My chest ached. I stood there, bent over, panting, gasping, choking in breath after breath.

A short while later, I felt a hand on my shoulder. I pulled myself up and saw that the three kids had followed me.

Kwame rolled his eyes. "That went well!" he said sarcastically.

"Kelly—why did you do that?" Gordon demanded. "You made a very bad impression on Skwerm."

"Why didn't you talk to him?" Penny May asked.

"He—he's a *monster*!" I cried. My voice was hoarse. My throat hurt. I grabbed Gordon by the shoulders. "Why?" I shouted. "Why? Why is there a monster in the school?"

All three of them squinted at me. No one answered for a long moment.

"How tiny *was* your school?" Gordon said finally.

Penny May scratched her head. "You didn't have a school monster? Seriously?"

"That's impossible," Kwame said.

"Every school in the state has a monster in the boiler room," Gordon said. "Did you really go to a school without a monster?"

"Uh . . . yeah," I said. "I—"

"Skwerm made all-state last year," Kwame said. "He's ranked in the top five school monsters every year."

"Skwerm is the best!" Penny May gushed. "The *best*!"

"They're always bragging about Burrrph over at the Madison Academy," Gordon says. "But Skwerm can eat Burrrph for lunch. Burrrph totally sucks."

My head spinning, I started to walk home. I wanted to get as far away from the school as I could. I had to think about this. I had to think hard.

The others trotted to catch up to me. "Listen,

Kelly," Gordon said. "You have to find a way to get on Skwerm's good side."

"You could be in major trouble," Penny May said. "I mean, you're at the bottom of the Tournament, Kelly. You're probably going to be Skwerm's date for Friiight Night."

"A lot of his dates don't look so good when the night is over," Kwame said. "You'd better think about that."

"Uh . . . okay," I said with a shudder. "I'll think about that."

12

"Dad, I have to change schools," I said.

He looked up from his laptop. I heard a lot of *beep*s and *boop*s. He's obsessed with this ancient *Space Invaders* game. He says it's good for his hand-eye coordination. Whatever that means.

He squinted at me. "What did you just say?"

"I said I have to change schools. Right away."

"What's that about?" Mom stepped into the den. "You just came from your school."

"I know," I said. "I have to get out of there. Adams Prep has a monster in the basement."

"We heard about that," Dad said. He still had his eyes on the laptop screen.

"It's very exciting," Mom said. "You get to have so many new experiences in a big school."

"Huh?" I gasped. "Did you hear what I said? There's an enormous monster in the school."

"You don't have to shout," Dad said. "We hear you."

"Just think," Mom said. "Now you get to show your brave side."

"Who says I have a brave side?" I cried.

They both laughed. They thought I was joking.

I uttered an angry growl. "So can I go to another school?"

"No way," Dad said. "Your mom and I studied all the schools here. Adams Prep was the best."

"You're lucky they took you in the middle of the year," Mom added.

"Lucky?" I said. "Lucky? I'll be lucky if I'm not *eaten alive*!"

"Don't exaggerate," Mom said.

Dad went back to his ancient video game.

Why didn't they get it? *Why?* Talking to them was like talking to a tree. Why didn't they understand how serious this was? Life and death! That's pretty serious.

I called Charlene. I knew she'd understand why I was so worried.

I told her about Skwerm. "He's as big as an elephant. He has blue warts on his face and ... and mushrooms growing on his shoulders. His teeth are pointy. He stinks to high heaven ..."

She listened to my whole description. Then she said, "And those are his *good* qualities?"

I couldn't help myself. That made me laugh. Charlene can always make me laugh.

"It's no joke," I told her. "He hated me immediately. I think he wanted to eat me right there and then."

"So what did you do?"

"Ran for my life," I said. "But I have to find a way to make him like me. If I don't, I'm going to be monster meat."

Charlene was silent for a long moment. I could almost hear her thinking over the phone. Finally, she said, "Why don't you juggle for him? He might like that."

"He's a vicious beast," I replied. "He isn't going to like juggling."

"Hmmm . . ."

"He's a roaring animal, like a movie monster, only bigger. And did I mention how bad he smells?"

"Bring him some deodorant," Charlene said, "as a gift. Maybe he'll appreciate that."

I rolled my eyes. "You're a riot," I said. And then I gasped. "Oh. Wait. You just gave me an idea."

13

I sat down in my room and Googled *school monsters* on my laptop. I wanted to learn as much as I could about them. An idea had flashed into my mind as I talked with Charlene. I wanted to make sure I was on the right track.

Google had a lot of suggested websites for me. I tried Monsterpedia, and it was very helpful. I also spent time on a website called School Monsters Center for Education and Health.

What did I learn?

Well, I learned that just about every large school in the state had a school monster living in the basement. Of course, that's what Gordon and the other kids had already told me. But it was hard to believe.

Why do the schools house monsters in their basements? To keep the boilers running all winter. And to act as guards to keep the school buildings safe. A chart showed that monsters make better guards than dogs or humans.

According to the monster info website, school monsters are allowed to leave the basement once a year, usually in the spring. They are allowed upstairs for a party called Friiight Night.

Different schools have different rules for Friiight Night. Most schools have a date for the monster at the party. Someone to hang out with the monster and take care of it. And see that it has a good time.

Monsterpedia had a special section called "Life of the Party."

It said that it doesn't happen very often. But once in a while, a monster loses control on Friiight Night and eats one of the students. Usually, the monster eats its date.

The website said that only happens ten percent of the time. That means that ninety percent of kids return home safely after the party.

So schools think it's worth keeping Friiight Night. It keeps the monsters happy and working the rest of the year.

Ninety percent didn't sound like a great number to me. In fact, reading it sent a shiver down my back. I knew who would be in the unlucky ten percent— Kelly Crosby. Me.

I read pages and pages about school monsters on a few more websites. But none of them told me what I wanted to know.

"Maybe Gordon knows," I said to myself.

The next morning, I walked over to his house. I told him what I was looking for, and he was very helpful.

Or so I thought.

14

Gordon lived in a long, low house on the edge of a lake. A wooden dock stretched into the lake. A small white boat bobbed in the water, tied to the edge of the dock.

As I walked closer, I saw Gordon sitting at the wheel of the boat. He waved when he saw me.

I hurried along the dock. The boards moved beneath my shoes. Gordon stuck out his hand and helped me lower myself into the boat.

"This is awesome," I said. "Do you take this around the lake?"

"I'm not allowed to take it out on my own," he replied. "But my dad likes to see how fast he can get it going, and he takes me along."

"So what are you doing now?" I asked.

"Just sitting in it," he said. "I like to sit in it. The way it bobs up and down is very relaxing. Helps me think."

"What are you thinking about?" I asked.

He shrugged. "I don't know."

"You're probably wondering why I came over," I said.

39

"Not really," he answered.

The boat tilted up under the wake from a passing boat and I grabbed the sides. "Well, I came for some advice," I said. "I thought maybe you could help me."

"Maybe," he said. He brushed a fly off his cheek. "What's it about?"

"It's about Skwerm," I said. "I want to give him a gift."

Gordon squinted at me. "Seriously?"

"Yes. I want to give him something to make him like me."

Gordon thought about it for a moment. "That could work," he said. "If you end up being his date on Friiight Night, you'll want him to be in a good mood. Or else . . ." He didn't finish his sentence.

I felt a chill. Was it just the cool wind off the lake?

"So what should I bring him?" I asked. "What would make a good gift? Do you have any ideas?"

Gordon shut his eyes and went silent for a long time. Finally, he opened them again and turned to me. "I know," he said. "Bring him eggs."

"Eggs?"

He nodded. "Skwerm loves eggs, Kelly."

"Awesome," I said. "That's easy."

The boat bobbed sharply. I gripped the sides harder.

"Here's what you do," Gordon said. "Take a dozen eggs and break them into a big bowl. Then whip them up until they're a thick yellow goo. Bring it to him for breakfast. Skwerm will like you for sure."

"Cool," I said. "Do I have to cook them or anything?"

He shook his head. "No need. Just bring him a bowl of whipped-up eggs."

"Hey, thanks, Gordon," I said. I stood up. The boat rocked from side to side. I started to tumble into the water. But he caught me and held on to me until my legs were steady. "Thanks for the help," I said, climbing onto the dock. "See you in school on Monday."

I hurried home, thinking about my gift for the monster. I told Charlene about it, and she thought it was a good idea.

On Monday morning, I woke up early. I went to the kitchen before Mom or Dad was awake.

I pulled a dozen eggs from the fridge and carried them to the counter. Then I cracked them into a big bowl. I was mixing them with a whisk when Dad wandered in.

He peered into the bowl. "Kelly, what's up with the eggs?" he asked.

"Uh . . . it's a science experiment for Ms. Waxman's class," I told him.

"Eggs are very interesting," Dad said, pouring ground coffee into the coffee maker. "Do you know who invented them?"

"No. Who?" I replied.

He frowned. "That was a joke, Kelly."

"Sorry," I said. "You need to warn me when you're going to make a joke."

I gulped down a bowl of cornflakes. Then I poured the eggs into a glass container, put the lid on, and hurried out the door. I couldn't wait to get to school.

It was very early. I didn't see anyone else heading into the building.

I gripped the container tightly as I slid in through the side door. The hall was empty. No one around. I made my way to the basement door.

"Skwerm, you're going to love this," I murmured to myself. "And you're going to love me. I hope."

I pulled open the door and started down the stairs.

15

The air grew warmer as I neared the basement. Gray morning light washed in from tiny windows along the ceiling.

I carefully took the last steps, cradling the container between my hands.

I squinted into the dim light. The enormous boiler threw a long shadow over the concrete floor. I didn't see Skwerm. But I could hear his heavy breaths, scratchy from deep in his throat.

I knew he was on the other side of the furnace.

"Skwerm . . . I brought you something." My voice came out shrill and tight. My legs started to tremble. The container slid from my shaking hands, but I caught it before it fell.

After a few seconds, I heard him stir. Then I heard a soft groan, a sigh, and heavy footsteps. His wide shadow rolled over the floor before he appeared.

I gasped as he burst out from behind the furnace. He was taller than I remembered. His eyes studied me, and then he opened his mouth in an angry roar.

"I know," I said. "You remember me." He roared

again, as if answering. He snarled, baring his huge teeth, and waved a menacing paw at me.

Gripping the container tightly, I took a step back to the wall.

What am I doing here? I asked myself. *This is a BIG mistake.*

Skwerm rose up even higher. Was he planning to attack?

I removed the lid, pushed the container out in front of me, and raised it toward him. "L-look," I stammered. "I brought you a gift."

My whole body shaking, I held the container up to him. "You like eggs? Do you? Like eggs?"

My hands trembled so hard, the container tilted. And egg goo splashed over the monster's wrinkly feet. "Uh-oh."

Skwerm stared down at his feet. Then he raised his four red, angry eyes and glared at me.

What is going to happen now?

16

The monster raised his head and roared at the ceiling. The whole basement shook from the sound. My hands trembled. More egg splashed onto the monster.

I tried to back away. But my legs refused to move.

With another roar, Skwerm wrenched the container from my hands. He raised it high. Turned it over . . .

"Ohhhh." I moaned as the egg goo plopped onto my head. I stood there gasping as it oozed down my face and over my shoulders.

Skwerm pulled his arm back and sent the empty container crashing against the basement wall. It hit with a deafening *THUD* and shattered into a thousand pieces.

I didn't wait to see what happened next. I spun around and finally forced my legs to do their job. I leaped up the stairs, taking them two at a time. I didn't run—I *flew*!

Egg slid down over my eyes. The sticky yellow goo stuck to my cheeks. I could feel it in my hair.

Gasping for breath, I reached the top of the stairway. I stumbled out into the hall and slammed the basement door behind me.

I lowered my hands to my knees, kept my head down, and struggled to catch my breath. "That went well," I told myself.

I stood up and tried to brush the hair that had fallen over my eyes. And now my hands were covered in the sticky egg goo.

It was still early. But a few kids had started drifting into school. Two girls stopped to stare at me. "What happened to you?" one of them asked.

"An accident," I said.

"Did you throw up your breakfast?" the other one asked.

"I wish," I said.

They turned and walked away.

Then I spotted Gordon, coming into the hall, pushing his pack on wheels in front of him. "Hey—!" I called. "Hey—!" I took off running to him.

His eyes opened wide. "Kelly? What's up?"

"I-I—" I just stood there stammering. I couldn't get any words out.

"You're early," he said.

Didn't he notice that I was covered in yellow goo?

"I took your advice," I finally managed to choke out. "And . . . and look at me. The monster took the eggs I brought him and poured them over my head."

Gordon stood open-mouthed. As if he didn't understand the words I was saying. Then after a long moment, he slapped his forehead. "Oh, right," he said. "He doesn't like eggs. I knew there was something about Skwerm and eggs. He's allergic to them. I forgot."

I stood squinting hard at him, my fists curled at my sides.

"My bad," he said. He shrugged. Then he pushed his pack and rolled past me down the hall.

Gordon is not my friend.

That was my first thought.

I'm in major trouble. The monster hates me now.

That was my second thought.

And then I asked myself a question:

Is there anything I can do to save myself?

17

I texted Charlene after school, and she called me back. "So what happened with the eggs?" she asked.

"You don't want to know," I answered.

"You mean—?"

"Gordon was the one who told me to bring eggs to the monster. And he knew Skwerm was allergic to them. Gordon just wanted to save himself. I think all the kids in school will do *anything* not to be chosen as the monster's date."

"So why do you think it will be you?" she demanded.

I sighed. "I just know it. I'm the new kid. Ms. Waxman told me I'm at the bottom of the Tournament. The monster hates my guts . . ."

She was silent for a while. "Any chance you can change schools?" she said finally. "Did you tell your mom and dad about this?"

"They think it's exciting," I replied. "They think it's a great opportunity."

"To be eaten alive by a monster?"

"To show how brave I am," I said. I sighed again. "I don't believe it, Charlene. But Friiight Night might be my first—and last—date in my entire life."

"Stop sighing like that," Charlene scolded. "You have to look on the bright side, Kelly."

"What's the bright side?" I demanded.

"It isn't happening to *me*!" she said.

We both cracked up laughing.

But what was there to laugh about?

Ms. Waxman said she would name the monster's date tomorrow.

And I knew his name would be spelled *K-E-L-L-Y*.

18

I tried bringing up the monster problem again at dinner.

Mom made a big bowl of spaghetti with Dad's special tomato sauce. He's very proud of his sauce and won't let anyone watch when he makes it.

I think that's because he gets it out of a can. But I would never say that out loud.

One day, I saw three or four cans of spaghetti sauce in the trash. Dad said those were just "starter" sauces.

"Would you like it if the school monster ate me on Friiight Night?" I asked.

Dad twirled spaghetti on his fork. Mom pointed to me. "You have tomato sauce on your chin."

I wiped it with my napkin. "What's the answer?" I said.

"There's still some on your cheek," Mom said.

"Forget the spaghetti sauce!" I cried. "This is serious!"

"We don't shout at the table," Dad said, still twirling his spaghetti.

I gritted my teeth and uttered a low *grrrrr.* "You

wouldn't like it if the monster ate me, right?" I tried again.

"We'd hate it," Mom answered. "We'd really miss you."

"If you are chosen, it's an honor," Dad said.

I jumped to my feet. "An honor? An *honor*? To be eaten alive by the school monster?"

"You'd be representing your school," Dad said.

"Huh? You think I should *die* for my school?"

"Don't be so grim," Mom said. "Why do you always have to be so grim?"

"Because being eaten alive is grim," I said. I dropped back to my chair. "Can I ask you one more time about taking me out of this school?"

"How would that help?" Mom asked. She spooned more salad onto her plate. "Every school has a monster. And every school has a Friiight Night."

"I hear the monster at Madison Academy is a real killer," Dad said.

"Is that supposed to cheer me up?" I replied.

Dad patted the back of my hand. "You need to relax," he said. "You know what I always say: Go with the flow."

"The flow?" I cried. "The flow? What does that even mean?"

He shrugged. "I don't know. But you should go with it."

That ended the conversation.

The next morning, I walked as slowly as I could to school. I took my place at the back of Ms. Waxman's class.

And I waited for my name to be called.

19

"This was a difficult year to choose," Ms. Waxman said.

She sat on the edge of her desk, twirling her eyeglasses in her hands. I think she was kind of stressed. She twirled them one way, then twirled them the other.

"I know the truth," she said. "I know you all have a bad attitude about being the monster's date."

You got THAT right, I thought.

"But," she continued, "you have to realize that it's a real honor to be picked."

Whoa. She sounds just like my dad.

She set the glasses down on her lap. "I'll tell you an actual fact," she said. "Over the years, ever since schools started keeping monsters, ninety percent of the Friiight Night dates have survived the night."

The room stayed silent. No one made a comment. No one made a sound. I realized the other kids were all as worried and scared as I was.

"Ninety percent," Ms. Waxman repeated. "That means you have a very good chance of staying alive through Friiight Night."

Again, silence. No one moved.

I felt my throat tighten. I had to force myself to breathe.

"Now, let me announce Skwerm's date." She turned and reached for a stack of papers on her desk. Squinting at them, she shuffled through several pages.

Why is she keeping us in suspense?

My hands were ice cold. I clasped them together to keep them from trembling. I clamped my jaw shut. My teeth were actually chattering.

Please don't pick me . . . Please don't pick me . . .

I glanced to the front and saw Gordon watching me. He was staring hard at me, and he had a tight-lipped grin on his face.

Did he know something?

Did he know the monster's date was me?

Ms. Waxman put on her glasses and scanned a sheet of paper. "The student with the lowest quiz scores is this year's date for Skwerm," she said.

She rattled the paper in her hand.

I sucked in a deep breath and held it. I squeezed my hands together so tightly, they ached.

"This year's date is Erin Barnard," she announced.

20

I let out a long whoosh of air. It sounded like air rushing out of a balloon.

The room erupted in sighs and moans and cheers.

I can't believe my good luck! I told myself. *Poor Erin. Poor Erin. Lucky me!*

I leaped up and pumped my fists above my head in triumph. I saw Gordon and some other kids doing a happy dance in front of the chalkboard.

In the middle of the room, Erin Barnard let out a squeal. She jumped to her feet, waving a hand at Ms. Waxman.

It took a while for the class to settle down. Erin stood there, waving at the teacher till everyone got quiet.

"Ms. Waxman, did you forget?" Erin cried.

The teacher scratched her forehead. "Forget?"

"I *told* you last week," Erin said. "I won't be here for Friiight Night. Remember? My family is leaving on a vacation to Barbados that day."

Ms. Waxman snapped her fingers. "Oh, wow," she said. "I *did* forget. I'm sorry, Erin. I forgot all about that."

"We'll be gone that whole week," Erin said. She dropped back into her seat.

"So sorry, Erin," Ms. Waxman said.

She picked up the sheet of paper and studied it. The room grew silent again. So quiet, I could hear everyone breathing.

"Since Erin can't be here," Ms. Waxman said, studying the sheet of paper, "Skwerm's date for Friiight Night will be Kelly Crosby."

21

Ms. Waxman asked me to stay after school. "We need to take care of some business," she said.

I didn't like the sound of that.

She pulled a tape measure from her desk drawer and had me stand up straight in the front of the room. Then she measured me from head to foot.

"Are you measuring me for a coffin?" I said.

She laughed and slapped me on the back. "You really are funny, Kelly," she said. "Where did you get your sense of humor?"

"From fear?" I answered.

She laughed again. "Follow me," she said. "I'll show you why I'm measuring you."

She led the way into the hall. Most of the kids had left. A few were closing up their lockers. No one looked at me when we passed. Maybe they felt too bad for me to look my way.

Ms. Waxman led me to the lunchroom. The room was empty except for one of the maintenance guys mopping the floor. "The pantry is back here," she said.

We walked into a narrow hallway beyond the kitchen. Two tall, shiny metal freezers stood tucked into the wall.

"Are we having an afternoon snack?" I said. I always joke when I'm scared to death.

She snickered. "No. I want to show you what you'll be wearing on Friiight Night."

"Uh . . . wearing?"

She nodded. She grabbed the handle to one of the freezers and pulled the door open.

A rush of cold air washed over me. I took a step back.

She pulled out a clothes hanger. It had some kind of outfit hanging on it. It was pink, covered in white frost. Frozen.

"We have to make sure it fits," the teacher said, holding it against my chest.

"I'm wearing f-frozen stuff?" I stammered.

She shook her head. "Of course not. We will thaw it out before Friiight Night."

"But—but—" I sputtered.

"It's a sweatsuit," she said. "Sweatpants and a sweatshirt. It's made of meat."

"Oh, sure," I said. "Now I get it. I always wear meat to parties."

"It's for safety," Ms. Waxman said. She held it up to me, then shoved it back into the freezer.

Safety? I didn't have a clue what she meant. I waited for her to explain.

"You see," she started, "we found out that sometimes Skwerm gets the nibbles during Friiight Night."

"N-nibbles?" I said. "You mean like, with his teeth?"

She nodded. "With his teeth."

I made a gulping sound.

"So we made a meat suit for his date to wear. If Skwerm gets hungry, he can chew on the suit and not on you."

My mouth dropped open. I couldn't think of anything to say.

"I'm glad you're thinking of my safety," I said finally.

"Well, we hate losing students on Friiight Night," Ms. Waxman replied. "It ruins the whole party."

"Wh-what if he finishes the meat suit?" I stammered. "And he's still hungry. Do you have any meat underwear for me to wear?"

She giggled. "We didn't think of that."

She checked to make sure the freezer door was closed. Then she pulled me by the hand. "Come along. One more important thing we have to do."

"One more? What's that?" I asked.

"We have to go see Skwerm."

22

I pulled my hand free and backed away from her. "I-I can't," I said. "I just remembered. I have an important appointment."

She squinted at me. "An appointment? What about?"

"I don't know," I said. "But it's important."

She shook her head. "It will only take a minute, Kelly. We just want to tell Skwerm the good news that you will be his date."

"I-I don't think it will be good news," I told her. "I already met him. He doesn't like me."

She grabbed my hand again and started to pull me toward the basement door. "No worries. You'll be totally safe because I'll be there to protect you."

"You'll protect me?" I said.

"That was a joke," she said. "Can't you tell when I'm joking?"

A blast of warm air hit me as she opened the basement door. My legs started to tremble and my heart did a few flip-flops in my chest.

She walked into the stairwell and pulled me down to the basement. I could hear the *hunnnh hunnnh*

hunnnh of the monster's breaths. And as I stepped beside Ms. Waxman on the basement floor, they grew a lot louder.

I huddled beside her. My legs felt so rubbery, I was afraid I might fall over. Flies buzzed somewhere. From behind the furnace, I think. The air felt heavy and wet and smelled sour like spoiled meat.

My lunch lurched up to my throat as the monster rumbled out from behind the furnace. His footsteps always sounded wet, a *squish squish* sound, as if his big paws were filled with water.

His eyes bulged when he saw me, and I knew he recognized me. He gnashed his teeth together, big jaws clicking loudly.

I heard Ms. Waxman gasp in surprise as the monster raised himself over me. He uttered a low growl. Opened his snakelike lips. And let a big ball of wet drool drip onto the top of my head.

"Owwww!" I cried out. Skwerm's drool was *burning hot.*

The monster raised his head and made a shrill *skeee skeee skeee* sound. I think it was monster laughter.

I rubbed my hair and my hands got covered in the hot drool.

The room seemed to darken as Skwerm raised his head over me again. I guessed he was preparing to let loose another drool bomb.

Ms. Waxman pulled me away just as the big gob came down. It smacked the floor with a loud *plop.* A heap of it splashed onto my shoes.

Skwerm let out another monster giggle—*skeee skeee skeee.*

60

"We have to go now," Ms. Waxman told him. "Kelly will see you at Friiight Night."

She gave me a push toward the stairs, and I took off running. I took two stairs at a time, stumbling on each step, but I didn't care.

When we reached the hall, Ms. Waxman slammed the door shut behind her. She waited as I stood there struggling to catch my breath.

Finally, she turned to me and patted my shoulder. "Kelly, you poor guy," she murmured. "That meat suit may be a waste of time. He seriously *hates* you."

23

"Maybe it won't be that dangerous, Kelly," Charlene said.

"Won't be dangerous?" I cried. "I should just say hello and stick my head in his mouth. Maybe I should rub peanut butter over my face to make it tastier for him."

I was in my room, hunched on the edge of my bed, after dinner. My hand squeezed the phone till my fingers throbbed. You might say I was a little tense.

"You always see the glass half-empty," she said.

I growled. "What does *that* mean? Why are you talking about a glass?"

"It's a saying," Charlene replied.

I growled again. "That monster hates me. I'm sure he's sitting behind the furnace right now, licking his lips."

"I'll bet they teach the monster to be polite on Friiight Night," Charlene said.

"Charlene, do you really think you can give a monster lessons in manners?"

Silence for a moment.

"Did you tell your parents?" she asked finally. "What did they say?"

"Mom was excited for me. Dad was proud of me."

"Do they know that the monster hates your guts?" she asked.

"I told them, but they don't believe it."

Another long silence.

"Maybe you could pretend to be sick that night," she said.

"Charlene, you know what a bad actor I am," I replied. *"No way* I could fool Mom and Dad. They're so excited for me, they'd drag me out of bed and take me to the party in my pajamas."

"Let's think of it from the monster's point of view," Charlene said.

"Why?"

"I don't know. But let's try it."

"What about his point of view?" I asked.

"Well . . . there he is all year long down in the basement by himself. And he's only allowed to come up and be with people one night a year . . ."

"So?"

"So I bet he gets really lonely down there," she replied.

"Whoa." I snapped my fingers. I slapped my forehead. "Charlene, you've just given me another idea! Why should Skwerm be lonely? Brilliant! Brilliant!"

24

At noon the next day, I found Erin Barnard in the lunchroom. She looked surprised when I sat down across the table from her.

I glanced at her lunch tray. A salad and a bag of pretzels.

"I try to take in the major food groups," she said.

"I'll bet Barbados is nice," I said. "Just saying."

She raised her right hand. "I swear, Kelly. We really are going. I didn't make it up."

At the next table, Gordon Willey was watching me. He had a big hero sandwich raised in front of him. But I could still see that he was grinning behind it. He took one hand off the sandwich to flash me a thumbs-up.

What was that guy's problem?

I turned back to Erin. "I know you're really going to Barbados," I told her. "But . . . because of that, I'm the monster's date."

She shoved a few pretzels into her mouth. "That's a shame," she said.

"Well, maybe you can help me," I said.

She swallowed the pretzels with a *gulp.* "Help you? How?"

I leaned across the table toward her. I stared into her eyes. "Maybe you can help save my life," I said.

She scrunched up her face. "Excuse me? Save your life?"

I leaned even closer and started to explain my idea.

SLAPPY HERE, EVERYONE.

Know what I think Kelly should do?

Spread mayonnaise over himself and climb between two slices of bread.

Because he's definitely going to be a monster's sandwich! Hahaha.

When Friiight Night comes, I don't think he'll be the life of the party! Especially since he's going to be on the dessert table for Skwerm. Haha.

Yes, he has a plan to save himself.

But when do those plans work out in *my* stories?

Like never! Hahaha.

Let's switch scenes now, folks. Let's check in with Charlene in Little Hills Village. She's having a big argument with her mom . . .

25

"I'm sorry, Charlene. But you can't travel to Great Newton, Massachusetts, by yourself."

"Well, you could come with me, Mom," I said.

"Huh? Why? Why on earth would I want to take off from work and travel to Great Newton?"

"Because Kelly is in trouble."

"If he's in trouble, he has parents to help get him out of it," Mom insisted.

I was helping her make the guest room bed, and we had the sheet sideways. She turned it one way, and I turned it the other.

"Charlene, you're not helping," she said.

"Because I'm pleading with you," I replied.

"You know I hate it when you plead." She chuckled. "You're not even a very good pleader."

I dropped my end of the sheet onto the mattress. "This isn't funny, Mom. It's serious. Kelly's parents aren't helping him."

Mom sighed. "We were good friends for a lot of years, Charlene. I know them. I know they wouldn't let Kelly get in serious trouble."

I rolled my eyes. "Serious trouble? Don't you think getting eaten by a school monster is serious trouble?"

Mom tucked her end of the sheet under the mattress. She motioned for me to pull my end into place. "Your school is too small to have a monster," she said. "But I watched a video about them the other day. They don't eat kids. They're very well trained. I think they even have a union."

"What's a union?" I asked. I didn't wait for her to answer. "Just listen to me—for once!" I cried.

"Charlene, don't shout at me."

"Kelly is the monster's date for Friiight Night at his school. And Kelly made the monster angry. He knows the monster hates him. You've got to believe me, Mom. Kelly is in a lot of danger."

She chewed her bottom lip. "Should I call Anna?"

I shook my head. "His mom won't help. She thinks it's exciting that Kelly was picked. She and Mr. Crosby don't understand the danger."

"Please tuck your end in. We can't spend all day on one sheet."

"You owe me a trip, Mom. Remember? My birthday trip that we didn't go on?"

Mom groaned. "Charlene, it wasn't my fault you had a hundred-and-three-degree fever that morning. You were sick."

"I wasn't sick. I just had a little fever. I could have gone."

She blew air through her lips. "Come on. What are we arguing about here?"

"About me going to help Kelly on his Friiight Night," I said. "About me helping to save his life."

"I'm really sorry," Mom said. "But if he is going to be eaten by the school monster, what can you do about it?"

"I-I'll think of something," I stammered. "Mom, I'll take the bus and—"

She shook her head so hard, I thought it might fall off. "No. No way." Then she grabbed my hand and held it. "Listen to me, Charlene. Kelly is going to be fine. Perfectly fine."

26

Well, here I am. Just call me Mr. Monster Meat. It's the night before Friiight Night. My whole class is in the gym, working hard to put up decorations and make it look like a real party.

A scary party.

Mr. Harrison, the custodian, helped us hang long streamers from the gym rafters. Someone brought in a life-sized statue of King Kong. They put it in the center of the gym and floated balloons from his enormous arms.

It turned out that Gordon is a *Star Wars* freak. He brought in big posters of Jabba the Hutt and other creatures from the movies. We covered one wall with them.

They are awesome-looking monsters—if you happen to like monsters. Which I don't, of course.

Erin and I stayed by the gym doors, working a helium tank to inflate black balloons. I couldn't stop my hands from shaking, and some of the balloons blasted off the machine before they were finished and flew across the gym.

Yes, I was stressed. Do I even have to say it?

Across the gym, a bunch of kids worked to hang a big banner on the wall. It read: *have a fright on friiight night* in tall, black stenciled letters.

Trust me. I didn't need anyone to tell me to have a fright.

When someone put a hand on my shoulder, I jumped a mile in the air.

It was Ms. Waxman. She laughed. "Sorry, Kelly. Did I scare you?"

I shook my head. "No. I was already scared," I said.

She motioned around the gym. "It's starting to look like a party," she said.

I didn't say anything. What could I say?

Her eyes locked onto mine. "Is there anything else you'd like us to do? Anything that would make you feel more comfortable?"

"Well . . . going back to Little Hills Village would make me more comfortable," I said.

It was her turn not to say anything.

"We're very proud to have a monster like Skwerm," she said finally. "Some kids are going to give short speeches about what a first-rate monster he is."

"Yeah. He's a real beauty," I muttered.

Ms. Waxman turned to Erin. "It's so nice of you to come help decorate even though you won't be able to be here tomorrow night."

"I like blowing up balloons," Erin said.

"Well, keep at it," the teacher said. "Skwerm loves pulling the balloons down and stepping on them."

"I'll bet he does," I said. A shiver ran down my back. "What else does he like to step on?"

Ms. Waxman chuckled. "Kelly, I see you're not quite in a party mood yet," she said.

"Not quite," I replied.

I heard some cries from across the gym. I turned and saw that the big banner had tilted off the wall.

Ms. Waxman spun around and hurried to help put it back up.

"This is our chance," I said to Erin. I started to the gym door. "Let's go."

Erin held back. "Are we really doing this?"

I nodded. "Yes. We're really doing this."

I pushed open the double doors and we slipped out of the gym.

27

We stepped out into a warm spring night. The air smelled like fresh-cut grass. A pale sliver of a moon hung low in the night sky.

We walked quickly to the street. A group of kids from the upper school huddled in the parking lot, just hanging out.

I don't think they saw us.

We trotted across Oak Street and kept walking, trying to keep in the shadows.

"What makes you think this has a chance of working?" Erin asked.

"It has to," I said. "You know my life depends on it." I shook my head. "I can't sleep. I can't eat. It's all I think about."

"Poor guy," she said. "So you've been totally stressed all week?"

"I've been juggling nonstop," I told her. "Juggling calms me down a little. Gives me something to concentrate on."

"Whatever works," she said.

We stopped at the corner. An SUV filled with teenagers rumbled by.

"Two more blocks to Madison Academy," Erin said, pointing. Then she squinted hard at me. "Why am I helping you?"

"Because you feel sorry for me," I said. "Because you know it could have been you instead of me."

She nodded. "I guess."

We started walking again.

"I'll think of you tomorrow when I'm on the beach in Barbados," she said.

"That doesn't cheer me up at all," I replied.

A bird let out a loud *caw* right over my head, and I jumped. "Don't those birds ever sleep?" I cried.

She squeezed my hand. "Chill."

Madison Academy came into view. It was a tall stone building with twin towers, one on each end. Two round windows near the roof appeared blacker than night. They looked like eyes watching us as we came near.

I shuddered. The building walls glowed an eerie green in the pale moonlight. A low stone wall surrounded it.

"Looks more like an evil castle than a middle school," I said.

Erin didn't reply. She was staring up at the two windows at the top.

A burst of warm air ruffled my hair. I turned and led the way to the side of the building. I could hear my blood pulsing in my ears. The only other sound was the crunch of our shoes on the gravel walkway.

Be brave, Kelly. I kept repeating those words as we walked. *Be brave, Kelly.*

I climbed over the low wall, turned, and helped Erin over it. Her hands were ice cold. I realized she was scared, too.

The lights were on in the back of the school. "That's the gym," I whispered. "I studied a map of the school."

"They must be decorating their gym for Friiight Night, too," Erin said.

I nodded. "I'm counting on it. That's part of the plan."

I stepped up to a narrow side door. Erin tugged me back. "Maybe we should forget this idea," she whispered. "I don't think we stand a chance—"

"Of course we do," I whispered back. "They're all busy in the gym. No one will see us."

"But—but—" she sputtered. Her eyes were wide with fear. Another gust of warm wind sent her hair flying. She tugged it down with both hands.

"We'll head right to the basement," I said. "I know where the stairs are."

"B-but it's so dangerous," she stammered.

"Not as dangerous as me being Skwerm's party favor," I said. "Follow me. We can do this."

I gripped the metal handle to the narrow door, pulled it open—

—and SCREAMED.

A huge man—a school guard in a red-and-gray uniform with a big gold badge on the front—blocked the doorway.

"Oh noooo. We're *caught*!" I cried.

28

Erin let out a scream, too.

I jumped back and toppled into her. Tangled together, we stumbled from the doorway.

The guard stared straight ahead, hands on his waist, and didn't move.

His face came into focus in the pale light. His eyes . . . his lips . . . they were *painted* on.

"He—he isn't real," Erin stuttered. "He's a dummy, a mannequin. You know. Like in clothing stores."

I let out a long whoosh of air. My heart was beating so hard, I think my T-shirt was bouncing with it.

I reached out with a trembling hand and slid it down the guard's painted face. "It's papier-mâché," I said.

"They probably put him here to fool intruders," Erin said.

"Well, we're intruders," I said, "and he fooled us."

She hung back. "Are we still going through with this?"

"We have to," I said. I bumped the mannequin out

of the way and stepped into the dark hallway. "We don't have a choice, Erin."

"Of *course* we have a choice," she said.

I waved her forward. "Come on. Hurry. The sooner we go downstairs—"

"I have to tell you something," she said. "Maybe I'm too scared."

"Too scared? But—"

"Kelly, do you know why my parents scheduled our trip to Barbados for tomorrow? Because they know I am terrified of Skwerm, and they wanted to rescue me from Friiight Night."

"Okay . . ." I said.

"The vacation wasn't an accident," Erin said. "My parents wanted to save me from him."

"Okay," I said again. "And now you're saving me from Skwerm. So let's go and—"

"I'm not so sure that kidnapping the Madison Academy monster is the way to save you," she said.

"It's my only plan," I told her. "My only chance." I grabbed her hands and pulled her into the hallway. "No more discussion, okay? It's time for action. I need you to help me. I might not be able to do it by myself."

She lowered her head and didn't reply. But she followed behind me as I made my way down the dark hall.

I had spent days studying the map of Madison online. I knew that the basement stairs were past the library, right after a left turn into another hall.

I could hear music and kids laughing from the gym. The sounds echoed in the empty hall.

I stopped in front of the basement door. My whole body was trembling. I turned to Erin. "We can do this."

She still didn't speak. She was looking down. Her hair had fallen over her face, but she made no effort to push it back.

"We can do this," I repeated. I figured if I kept saying it, maybe I'd believe it.

Was it a totally crazy idea? To kidnap Burrrph and take him to our school to meet Skwerm?

Maybe. But it was my only idea.

I gripped the doorknob and pulled the basement door open. I peeked into the stairwell. A dim bulb hanging from the ceiling sent yellow light down the steep metal stairs. Pale light washed over the basement floor far below.

"Follow me," I whispered to Erin. I stepped onto the top stair. Wrapped my hand around the metal railing. Took one step down. Then another.

I turned and saw that Erin was right behind me.

I stopped when I heard a deep groan from down below. Heavy *thud*s. Footsteps. Another groan.

"He's down there," I whispered. My mouth was so dry, the words caught in my throat.

I gripped the railing tighter and took another step down.

"Ohhhh!" A cry escaped my throat as a deafening *ROOOOOOAAAAARRR* exploded from the basement. So loud, it made the railing shake and the stairs tremble beneath my shoes.

"It—it—it's Burrrph," I stammered to Erin.

I turned and saw her back. She was running.

Running full speed up the stairs, her shoes slamming on the metal steps.

"I'm outta here, Kelly!" she cried. "Sorry. But I'm outta here!"

"No, wait—" I reached for her. But she was too far away to grab. "Erin—don't! Come back!"

I dove forward and nearly toppled off the step. "Come back! I need you!"

I stumbled up the stairs after her. Into the dark hall. "Come back!" I forced my legs to move as I chased after her. "Please, Erin—!"

She lowered her shoulder, shoved the door open, and disappeared outside.

I caught the door before it slammed in my face and followed her out. "Erin—stop! Please—!"

She didn't look back. I watched her race to the street. Then she turned and fled up the block.

Gasping for breath, I stopped. I lowered my hands to my knees and struggled to breathe. I could still hear her pounding footsteps down the block.

Shaking my head, I stood up and turned to the school building. *How can I do this by myself? How could Erin let me down?*

Easy!

Now what?

And that's when someone grabbed me hard.

Wrapped their hands around my waist.

And spun me around.

And I let out a startled scream.

29

"Noooo! Charlene! What are you doing here?"

I stared at my friend in shock. She let go of me, and a wide grin spread over her face.

Charlene laughed. "Surprised you, huh? You should see the look on your face." Her green eyes flashed in the moonlight. Her long coppery hair glowed around her face like some kind of halo.

"How? Where? What?" I blinked at her, trying to get myself together.

"I'm not a ghost," Charlene said. "You don't have to look so frightened."

"I-I'm not frightened," I stuttered. "Just shocked."

"It wasn't easy. But I convinced my mom to drive me," she said. "I knew you were in trouble, and—"

I tugged her hair. "You're real. You're really here."

She shoved my hand away. "Stop acting so weird. Aren't you glad to see me?"

"Y-yes," I stammered. "I—"

"I knew you were in trouble, so I came," she said. "I dropped off my bag at your house. Your mom said you were at school. I went there and saw you leave with that girl. I followed you here." She gazed up at the stone walls of Madison Academy. "What are you doing here, Kelly?"

I heard a burst of laughter from inside the gym. Then loud voices.

I pulled Charlene into the shadow of a tree. "I came to kidnap the school monster," I said. "But my helper chickened out."

Charlene squinted at me. "Was that the girl I saw running down the street?"

I nodded. "Erin. She was too afraid of the monster."

"Smart girl," Charlene murmured. "And what kind of weird plan made you want to kidnap a monster?"

"It was *your* idea," I told her. "I mean, you're the one who gave me the idea."

A gust of wind made her long hair shiver. The moon disappeared behind some clouds, and we were surrounded in darkness.

Charlene crossed her arms in front of her. "Kelly, I did *not* tell you to go kidnap a monster," she said.

I heard more voices from the gym. Some kids in there were applauding something.

Were they finished decorating? Were they about to come out?

"No time to explain," I whispered.

"If you want my help, you *have* to explain," she insisted.

"Okay, okay. You said Skwerm was probably lonely. Down in the basement by himself almost every day of the year. Remember?"

81

"I kind of remember that," Charlene said.

"Well, that gave me the idea to kidnap Burrrph, the Madison monster, and bring him to my school. He can be Skwerm's date for Friiight Night instead of me. It will be the most awesome Friiight Night in history! Two monsters. They'll be happy—and I'll be safe."

I waited for her to react. But she just stared hard at me.

Finally, she spoke up. "That's the dumbest thing I ever heard," she said.

30

"Kelly, really. It may be the dumbest thing I ever heard. But it just may work."

My mouth dropped open. "You think?"

She nodded. "You might make the two monsters very happy. And then they'll definitely ignore you."

I grabbed her hand and started to pull her to the side door. "The Madison kids are in the gym," I explained. "You know. Getting it ready for tomorrow night. The halls are empty. The coast is clear."

I held the side door open for her. She stayed back. "Do you know how to get to the basement?"

I nodded. "We were on our way down there when Erin decided she was too scared."

"Luckily for you, I'm not as smart as Erin," Charlene said. She stepped into the school and followed me down the hall. We crept as silently as we could, keeping in the shadow of the wall.

I heard cheers from the gym at the back of the school. I held my breath. What would we do if the Madison kids came pouring out? How could I explain what Charlene and I were doing here?

I pulled open the basement door, and we stepped

into the stairwell. My heart started to pound on the first step.

Charlene and I were halfway down when we heard the monster's low growl. We both stopped, gripping the rail tightly, and stared at one another.

The monster was moving around down there. I heard grunts and hard *thud*s and heavy, plodding footsteps on the basement floor.

My legs started to tremble. I had to force them to keep carrying me down the steep metal stairs. Behind me, Charlene was breathing rapidly.

I was two steps from the bottom when I saw Burrrph.

I gasped out loud. I'd expected a bearlike creature, tall and leathery like Skwerm. But this monster was way different.

He looked like a stingray. You know, one of those flat, rubbery ocean creatures you see in aquariums. Only, he stood straight up. He was at least eight feet tall!

Like a wet, gray blanket with eyes!

That was my first thought.

His round black eyes peered at us. Two bumps on top of his head that looked like human fingers waved like antennae. His entire body pulsed wetly, as if it were swimming underwater.

"Burrrph—" I managed to choke out his name.

He instantly stood tall. His whole body billowed, like waves rolling down his front. The stubby antennae on his head stood straight up. His round black eyes locked on me.

"Burrrph—"

84

Then a dark hole opened in the middle of the creature. His mouth!

The hole opened and grew wider ... wider ... I could see only darkness inside, like a deep black tunnel.

"Ohhhh ..." A groan escaped Charlene's mouth. She grabbed my shoulder as the huge creature rose up over us. The mouth was a gaping cavern-like opening now.

He uttered a roar. I felt a rush of burning hot air from his open mouth.

The monster leaned forward. He opened his mouth wider ... wider ...

"YAAAAIIII!" I screamed. "He's going to eat us BOTH!"

What had I been THINKING?

31

I staggered until my back hit the wall. "BURRRPH!" I screamed up at the monster as loud as I could. "BURRRPH—LISTEN TO ME!"

He hovered over us. The mouth hole in the middle of his body seemed to float over me.

"We have a date for you!" I cried in a shrill voice I'd never heard before. A voice of total panic. "A date for Friiight Night!"

Burrrph didn't move. His wet body pulsed. His gaze locked onto me.

"You don't have to be lonely," I shouted up at him. "If you come with us."

Another burst of hot air poured from the wide mouth hole.

Charlene jabbed my shoulder. "Kelly—what if he doesn't understand? What if he doesn't speak English?"

"W-wish I'd thought of that," I stammered.

"Huh?" Charlene bumped me again. "What else didn't you think of?"

"Well . . ."

"How did you plan to get him out of here?" She

couldn't hide the panic in her voice. "How are you going to get him out of this basement? Did you plan for two of us to take his hands and walk him to your school?"

"He doesn't have hands," I said.

I reached into my jeans pocket and tugged out the dog leash and collar I had brought. "I thought . . ."

"*That's* what you brought?" Charlene cried. "He's a giant stingray! He's eight feet tall! He has no arms or legs! You're going to walk him out of here with a dog leash?"

"I-I guess not," I murmured.

She grabbed my shoulder and tugged me toward the basement stairs. "We have to go, Kelly. This isn't going to work. We have to regroup."

"Huh? Regroup?"

Charlene didn't have a chance to answer.

Before she could move, Burrrph's wide body swooped down and wrapped itself around her. Like a shimmering, pulsing blanket, the monster folded himself around her.

Then he arched his whole body and raised Charlene high in the air.

"He . . . he's tightening . . . tightening . . ." Charlene choked out.

I couldn't see her. She was folded inside the monster.

"Can't breathe . . ." she gasped. "HELP me, Kelly! DO something!"

I froze.

Charlene's cries became muffled.

What could I do? I couldn't fight Burrrph. I knew I wasn't strong enough to pry him open so that Charlene could slip out.

"Put her down!" I finally found my voice. "Put her down—*now*!" I screamed.

He didn't budge.

Of course he didn't budge. Why would an eight-foot-tall monster be afraid of *me*?

"Kellll-eeee . . ." Charlene choked out my name.

The monster had her wrapped up as tight as a mummy. His body pulsed and made wet, squishy sounds.

Was it *digesting* her?

In my panic, my brain went blank. I dove forward, stretching my arms out to tackle the creature.

Burrrph made a grumbling sound. A low growl from deep inside his body.

I stopped myself. Regained my balance.

Think . . . Think . . .

My hands sank into my jeans pockets. I didn't think about what I was doing. I didn't even realize I was doing it.

I took out my three juggling balls. I squeezed them in my trembling hands.

My first idea was to heave them at the monster.

I raised one of the soft leather balls high. Pulled my arm back.

Then I stopped.

No way Burrrph would be afraid of a little juggling ball. No way it could hurt him or make him free Charlene.

I started to juggle the three balls. I was so terrified, I didn't even think about it.

I tossed them up slowly in front of me. Caught them one by one and sent them flying up again in a circle.

The monster shifted his weight. His eyes moved. Was he following the balls?

"Watch this!" I cried. I started to juggle faster. "Burrrph—watch this!"

His eyes moved with the balls. Yes! He was watching!

I tossed them higher, and he followed them as they bounced up from my hands.

He *was* watching. He was interested. *Now what?* I asked myself. *What do I do now?*

Zip. Zip. Zip. The balls slapped my hand and flew back up into the circle.

The monster kept his eyes on them. His body pulsed faster. It looked like waves rushing down him.

Now what? Now what?

I was so terrified, so frozen in fear, I dropped one of the balls.

It hit the basement floor with a soft *plop*. I let the other two balls drop to the floor beside it.

Hennnnnh. The monster made a weird sound, and his body quivered.

What was that? Was that laughter?

Was he laughing because I dropped the balls?

I scooped them up and began to juggle again. After a few seconds, I let one drop to the floor.

Hennnnnh. That sound again. Burrrph's body jiggled.

"He's laughing," I muttered to myself. "I know he's laughing."

I have his attention, I decided. *Maybe now he'll listen to me.*

I held the three balls high. "Let Charlene go!" I screamed. "Let her go—NOW!"

Would it work? Would he do it?

33

No.

He didn't move.

I gasped. "Charlene? Are you okay? Can you hear me?" I cried.

She didn't answer.

"Charlene?"

Silence.

"Oh nooooo." A moan escaped my throat.

I raised one of the juggling balls high. "Charlene?"

No answer.

With a desperate cry, I *heaved* the ball at the monster.

To my surprise, the monster opened up—and caught the ball in one fin.

Burrrph stretched himself wide—and Charlene came crashing to the floor.

I dove forward and bent down beside her. "Are you okay? Charlene?"

"I-I—" She sat up slowly. She rubbed her clothes with both hands. "I'm covered in goo!"

"Never mind that." I pulled her to her feet and away from the monster. Her hands were sticky from the monster goo. Her hair, drenched in it, stuck to her head.

I gave her a push, and she scrambled to the stairs.

Then I turned in time to see Burrrph toss the juggling ball back to me.

I made a stab for it. Missed. It sailed over my head and hit the wall.

Charlene was climbing the stairs. Her shoes made wet squishing sounds as she climbed.

I grabbed up the ball, turned back to Burrrph, and started juggling again. Once again, the round black eyes followed the balls as I tossed and caught them.

Keeping a steady pace, I started to back up. Juggling slowly, watching Burrrph the whole while, I inched my way to the stairs.

As I juggled, the monster moved forward. With heavy, wet steps, he followed me. His eyes never left the balls in the air.

I backed onto the first stair. Then the next.

Burrrph slid forward. Watching. His wide, flat body billowed as he moved, like a flag blown by the wind.

"Charlene—it's working!" I called up to her. "He's following me. It's working."

I held my breath. Would he really follow me up the stairs and out of the school? Would he really follow the juggling balls all the way to my school?

Charlene waited for me at the top of the stairs. We both watched the monster slide up after us, leaving a thick trail of goo behind him.

I could hear voices down the hall. Kids laughing. They were still in the gym. Still getting ready for their Friiight Night.

And what a surprising Friiight Night the Madison Academy kids were going to have. A Friiight Night party *with no monster*!

I stumbled on the top step. Caught my balance and kept juggling. I started down the hall to the side door.

And Burrrph followed. Grunting, his body sloshing, his eyes stayed on the balls as I tossed them in front of me.

I backed out the door. Charlene held it open as the monster lumbered after us. I turned around.

Clouds drifted over the moon. Trees in the schoolyard cast pools of darkness over the ground.

"It's so dark, I can't see anything," I murmured. "I can't juggle. I can't see the balls."

"Do your best," Charlene said, motioning with one hand. "Walk this way. I'll open the gate." She hurried ahead.

I heard the metal gate squeak open. I followed her out of the schoolyard. Burrrph grunted and growled as he made his way behind us.

I caught up to Charlene. "Can you believe this is working?" I said.

"So far, so good," she replied. "But what's next?"

"We lead the monster to my school," I said. "We take him down to the basement to meet Skwerm. They'll have time to get to know one another before the party tomorrow night."

We walked quickly along the curb. "You're not going to tell anyone about it?" she asked.

I shook my head. "No. It has to be a big surprise. For everyone."

We crossed the street and started onto Adams Boulevard. I glanced back to make sure Burrrph made the turn with us.

"Hey—Burrrph?"

I didn't see him.

Charlene spun around. "Where is he? I don't see him."

We both squinted into the heavy darkness.

"Burrrph? Hey, Burrrph?"

"Where is he? Where did he go?"

We both took off, trotting back the way we came.

"Burrrph! Burrrph!"

He was gone.

34

We searched for at least an hour with no luck. Frightened, worried, and exhausted, we returned to my house.

Mom and Dad were in the den watching the news on TV. They both looked up when Charlene and I entered the room.

"How did it go?" Mom asked. "The gym all decorated for Friiight Night?"

"All decorated," I said. "We're ready to party."

"Charlene, it's so nice to see you tonight. Did you have a good time at Kelly's school?" Mom asked.

"It—it was more exciting than I thought," Charlene said.

Good answer.

Suddenly, the TV news reporter caught my attention.

"Breaking news," he said. "The headmaster of Madison Academy has told local police that the school monster is missing. Students discovered this when a side entrance to the school was found open. A search of the basement revealed that the monster had escaped."

A photo of Burrrph appeared on the screen.

A man with short gray hair, wearing a dark suit, stepped forward. He was identified as Headmaster Crane. "I think this might be a Friiight Night prank. The basement door is always locked," he said. "The monster must have had help to escape."

I felt my throat tighten. I struggled to breathe.

"Who would do such a thing?" Headmaster Crane continued. "Who would ruin our tradition? Please— whoever you are—return our school monster."

I gasped. I suddenly felt sick. *Had anyone seen us? What will happen to us if we're caught?*

The news reporter returned. "Although the monster is extremely dangerous," he said, "police ask everyone not to panic."

35

I dragged Charlene into the kitchen. I pulled cans of soda from the fridge, and we sat down across from each other at the table.

"The whole town is in danger because of us," I said.

She frowned at me. "Don't say *us*. I think the whole thing was *your* plan."

"I couldn't have done it without you," I said. I popped the top off the soda can. "We can't waste time deciding who to blame, Charlene. We have to do something."

She spun the red can in her hands. "Do something? Like what? Should we text the monster? Tell him to please hurry home?"

"This is not funny," I said. "If someone gets hurt— or killed—it's our fault. We could be *murderers*!"

"That's so like you," Charlene said. "Always looking on the bright side."

I wanted to toss my soda can at her. "Didn't you come all this way to help me? Why aren't you helping me?"

She raised both hands. "Okay, okay. You're right. I always make jokes when I'm afraid." She raised the can and took a long drink. "Let's think. Where would an escaped monster go?"

"Maybe to the woods?" I said. "Burrrph hasn't had any fresh air in at least a year."

"Maybe to the lake?" Charlene said.

"There *is* no lake here," I told her.

"Well, how am I supposed to know that?" she snapped. She burped loudly. "I hate fizzy soda. Don't you have any juice?"

"How can you think about juice when there's a dangerous monster loose in town?" I said.

Mom poked her head into the kitchen. "I heard you," she said. "Did that news story about the escaped monster frighten you two?"

"A little," I said.

"Well, you shouldn't worry," she replied. "I'm sure the police department here has a trained monster-hunting squad. They'll take care of it in no time."

I stared at her. "Monster-hunting squad? You're making that up—aren't you?"

Mom nodded. "Yes, I am. I thought it might make you feel better."

She grabbed a bag of nacho chips from the cabinet and disappeared back to the den.

"I'll tell you one good thing," Charlene said. "Burrrph can't hide or blend in. People will notice him. He will be spotted right away."

"I guess that's a good thing," I replied. "But what happens when he's spotted?"

"You hurry to him and do your juggling magic," she said.

I blinked. "I do *what*?"

"Your juggling hypnotizes him," she said. "If you juggle for him, he'll follow you wherever you want to take him. We just have to make sure we don't lose him this time."

A hard knock on the kitchen door made me jump off my chair.

I froze.

Another loud *bang* sounded on the door.

Charlene and I stared at each other.

"It—it's the monster," I stammered. "He followed us."

Charlene gave me a push. "Go see."

I pulled the door open—and gasped.

36

"Gordon—what are you doing here?" I said.

He grinned and pushed past me into the kitchen without an invitation. "I wondered where you went," he said.

He headed to the fridge. "Do you have anything to drink? They ran out at school. We were all dying of thirst." He stopped when he saw Charlene. "Hey. Hi."

"Hey," Charlene said.

Gordon pulled open the fridge door and scanned the shelves.

Charlene pulled me aside. "Who is your friend?" she whispered.

"He isn't my friend," I whispered back. "I told you, he played that mean trick on me with the eggs. He's the reason Skwerm hates me."

She kept her eyes on Gordon. "So he's actually an enemy?"

"You might say that," I told her.

Gordon took a long drink from a soda can. "I saw you and Erin leave the gym early," he said, wiping his mouth with the back of his hand. "What's up?"

"This is my friend Charlene from back home," I said.

Gordon snickered. "Did you come to see Kelly get eaten by Skwerm tomorrow night at the party?"

"Yes," Charlene answered. "I want a front-row seat."

That made Gordon snicker even louder. I hated the way he snickered. It didn't sound like laughing. It sounded like he had something stuck in his throat.

"You didn't answer my question," he said. "About you and Erin." He took another long drink.

"We got bored. So we left," I replied. "Erin went home. Then Charlene showed up to surprise me. I wanted to show Charlene the town. She's never been here."

He studied her. "Are you missing your Friiight Night back in that little town where you live?"

"Our school is too small," Charlene said. "We don't have a Friiight Night."

"Too bad," Gordon said. "It's a great party." He turned to me. "Unless you're the monster's date."

"Kelly isn't afraid," Charlene said.

Gordon grinned again. "Yes, he is. He messed up with a bowl of eggs. And now the monster hates him."

"Kelly knows how to handle monsters," Charlene insisted.

Gordon's eyes flashed. "We'll see." He took another long drink, then crushed the can in his hand. He tossed the can into the sink.

"So what are you doing for fun while you're in town?" he asked Charlene. "Going bowling? Kelly always wants to go bowling."

I didn't give Charlene a chance to answer.

Bowling.

The word set off an explosion in my mind.

Bowling. Yes! *Bowling!*

Why hadn't I thought of it before?

37

Gordon followed us to the bowling alley on Frederick Street, two blocks from our school.

He kept demanding, "What are we doing? Why are we doing this? Where are we going?"

But I didn't answer.

I hoped I was right.

I hoped we would find the monster there.

We were near the bowling alley when we lost Burrrph. And I remembered the neon sign above the building. The sign with three flying bowling balls.

Burrrph was hypnotized by my juggling balls. Maybe the bowling balls on the sign had also put him in a trance.

I saw the crowd a block away from the building. People jammed the street. They were screaming and shaking their fists and shouting at each other.

Over the shouts of the crowd, I heard sirens in the distance.

And there stood Burrrph across from the bowling alley. He had his broad, flat back turned away from the screaming crowd. He was staring up at the bright neon sign high on the front wall.

The sign read BOWLING in tall black letters. And just as I remembered, three big bowling balls appeared to be flying over the top of the sign. As if they were being juggled in the air.

Burrrph ignored the crowd and gazed up at the flying bowling balls on the sign.

Gordon pulled my arm. "Let's get out of here!" he cried. "That monster is dangerous!"

And as he said it, Burrrph spun around. His black eyes went wide as he faced the crowd. He tilted his flat stingray head back and let out a furious roar.

The sound silenced the crowd. People fell back. Many turned and ran.

"He—he's going to attack!" Gordon cried, tugging my arm.

I raised a hand to quiet him. "Gordon—you can save the day," I shouted over another deafening roar from the monster. "You can be a hero."

Gordon's mouth dropped open. "Huh? Me? What are you *talking* about? We have to run. We have to—"

I shook him hard. "Listen to me," I said. "You can save everyone from the monster. You will be famous. The whole town will love you."

Gordon squinted at me. "What do I have to do?"

"I've studied Burrrph," I told him. "There's only one thing that will calm him down. One thing that can control him."

"Tell me," Gordon said. "Tell me. I'll do it, Kelly. I'm a natural-born hero. Really."

I leaned close and whispered in Gordon's ear. "Burrrph is a total sucker for 'Row, Row, Row Your

Boat,'" I told him. "The song puts him in a trance. I'm a terrible singer. I can't carry a tune. But if you sing it to him, he will go into a swoon."

Gordon squinted at me. "Seriously?"

I nodded. "Seriously. You can save the whole town, Gordon. Just walk up to Burrrph and start singing 'Row, Row, Row Your Boat.'"

Charlene overheard me. She grabbed me and spun me around. "Kelly—what are you doing? You know that's a total lie. Why—?"

"It's called payback," I told her. "Keep out of it."

"But—but—" she sputtered.

The monster raised himself high over the crowd and opened his mouth in another terrifying roar.

I turned back to Gordon. "Can you do it? Can you be a hero?" I demanded.

"Just watch me," he said.

He turned away from me. Pushed his way through a crowd of people. Strode up to Burrrph. Raised his face to the monster and began to sing at the top of his lungs.

"Row, row, row your boat
Gently down the stream . . ."

38

Gordon didn't get any farther.

Before the next "row, row, row," Burrrph leaned over, spread himself over Gordon, and lifted him high off the ground.

The crowd squealed and screamed as the monster wrapped itself around Gordon and folded him into its enormous rubbery body.

Gordon disappeared inside the monster in seconds.

I could hear him screaming in there. But I couldn't make out the words.

Charlene bumped me in the side. "Payback?" she said.

I nodded. "Payback."

She grabbed me by the shoulders. "Well, are you going to save him?"

I shrugged. "I guess."

I fumbled the juggling balls from my jeans pockets. Then I pushed my way through the clumps of horrified onlookers. I strode up to Burrrph. "Hey, watch!" I screamed to get his attention.

And I started to juggle.

At first, the big monster didn't react at all.

I heard muffled cries from Gordon. Burrrph had him wrapped up like meat inside a dumpling. I knew he probably couldn't breathe too well.

My juggling had to work—fast.

I tossed the balls higher. I tried to toss them as high as the monster's face.

Burrrph ignored my juggling and stared at the sign on the building.

"Hey—watch!" I shouted. "Burrrph—watch!"

But the shouts and cries from the horrified crowd drowned out my words.

Charlene grabbed my arm. "Do something! DO something!" she screamed.

Panic choked my throat. My hands trembled as I juggled.

What could I do? My mind spun like a merry-go-round.

Poor Gordon. What have I done?

"One last try," I murmured out loud.

I took one of the balls, raised it high—and bounced it off Burrrph's head.

39

The ball bounced off the monster's head and fell into my hand.

I tossed another ball up and bounced it off his chest.

Finally, the big creature turned toward me. My whole body shuddered as I watched him turn, and my breath caught in my chest.

Slowly, he started to unfold himself. Gordon slid out and dropped to the sidewalk. He was completely covered head to toe in thick slime. He landed on his back and didn't move.

"Gordon! Gordon—are you okay?" Charlene screamed.

He climbed to his knees. He shook his head, dazed. He rubbed slime from his face with both hands. Then he raised himself to his feet and took off running.

"Gordon! Gordon!" Charlene called after him.

But he disappeared into the crowd and never looked back.

"Now what?" she demanded.

I shrugged. "I don't know. At least I got his attention."

The monster stared down at me, his black eyes rolling in his flat stingray head. People screamed as he took a heavy step toward me.

I dropped one of the juggling balls. It started to roll away. But I grabbed it and balanced the three balls between my hands.

Then I raised my hands toward the monster and started to juggle again.

He stared at the balls as they flew in front of me. Then he took another big step closer.

I backed away, keeping the balls moving in the air.

He took another step. His eyes followed the balls.

I backed through the crowd. People screamed again and scattered in all directions as the creature lumbered forward.

"It—it's working!" Charlene stammered. "He's following you, Kelly!"

Yes. He was hypnotized by the juggling once again. And following me down the street as we left town.

"Where are you taking him?" Charlene asked, hurrying to keep up with us. "What is your plan?"

"Uh . . . plan?"

I realized I didn't know where we were going.

It was too late to take him to our school. The kids would have finished decorating the gym. Everyone would be home by now, and the school would be locked up.

"Well, you can't just keep juggling and walking all night," Charlene said.

"You're so wise," I said sarcastically. "Why don't you help me think of something instead of just asking me questions I can't answer?"

I turned onto Poplar Street and kept juggling.

Burrrph turned and followed, his eyes on the floating balls.

"I'm thinking, I'm thinking," Charlene said. "Should we return him to his school? Take him to the police? You could be a hero for returning him."

"No. No way," I said. "We've worked too hard. I don't want to give up my plan."

We were one block from my house.

My arms were starting to ache from juggling. I wondered what would happen if I stopped for a short while.

"Well . . . how about this? He could stay in your room tonight," Charlene said. "You could lock your door and—"

"*Are you KIDDING me?*" I cried. "I'm going to spend a night with a *monster*? Did you see what he did to Gordon?"

"Okay. Okay, Kelly. I'll keep thinking."

I moved to the curb as a large SUV rumbled by. The headlights rolled over Burrrph, then me. And then the car squealed to a stop.

A back window rolled down. "Hey—!" someone shouted from inside the car. "Hey—stop! That's the school monster from Madison! STOP!"

40

Caught.

I froze. The juggling balls dropped into my hands.

Charlene spun to the big SUV. Her eyes were wide with fright.

Burrrph appeared to freeze, too.

"Stop right there!" someone shouted from the car. A young man's voice. "Where do you kids think you're going with the school monster? He's dangerous!"

"I-I-I—" I couldn't speak.

The passenger door swung open. A young man burst out. He was tall and thin, dressed in black jeans and a black sweater. He wore a baseball cap sideways over his head. His face was hidden in shadow.

I could see two other people in the car. The headlights washed over the street.

The young man took a few steps toward Charlene and me. "How did you get that monster? You know you have to return it."

Before I could answer, Burrrph moved. He dove forward, rising taller. He seemed to expand, like a sponge filling with water. And his mouth opened until it became a gaping dark hole.

"AAAAARRRRRGGGGGGGHH!"

The roar that burst from the monster's open mouth shook the trees. The car headlights bobbed up and down. The ground beneath me seemed to shake.

My ears rang.

The young man let out a yelp. His legs started to fold. He spun around and grabbed the open car door.

Gripping the door, he swung himself into the car. A few seconds later, the door slammed shut. The car took off, the tires squealing, the engine roaring.

Charlene and I stood watching until it swerved around the corner and disappeared. We were both breathing hard.

I turned to Burrrph. "You're a scary dude," I said.

The monster stared at the juggling balls cupped in my hands.

"Those people will definitely call the police," Charlene said. "We don't have much time to hide him."

I nodded. "Okay, okay. We're just a block away from home. We'll hide him there."

"You can lock him in the basement," she said. "He's used to living in a basement."

"That might work," I said. "Then we'll bring him to school for the party."

I started to juggle again and began walking to my house. Burrrph followed, hypnotized by the flying balls.

"I can't believe I'm bringing a monster into my house," I told Charlene.

She shrugged. "What choice do you have?"

"Well," I said, "maybe *not* bring a monster into the house?"

She didn't reply. We had no other plan. We had to hide Burrrph till Friiight Night. My basement seemed the best place.

I opened the back door silently. Then I backed into the kitchen, juggling the balls in front of me. The monster had to duck his head to get through the door. But he followed the floating balls without stopping.

I led him down the hall to the basement stairs. Mom and Dad were in the den. I could hear voices on the TV.

"Kelly, is that you?" Dad called.

"Yes. We're home," I shouted.

The monster was bent over because of the low ceiling. He bumped the wall hard.

"What was that?" Dad called. "Did you fall?"

"Just kidding around with Charlene," I said.

The monster uttered a low growl.

"What was that?" Mom demanded.

"Uh . . . just my stomach growling," I said. "I guess I'm hungry."

"Should I get up and make you both something?" Mom said.

"NO!" I cried. "Please! Don't get up. Watch your show."

"We're okay," Charlene yelled. "No worries."

I pulled open the basement door and clicked on the

light. I motioned for Burrrph to follow me down the stairs. The big monster squeezed into the narrow stairway. He was so huge, he blocked out the light.

Oh no, I thought. *He's going to get stuck in the stairway. I'll never get out of here, and neither will he!*

But he slid down easily, leaving a trail of slime on the stairs.

I listened for my parents to come to the basement door. But all I could hear were the grunts and heavy, thudding footsteps of the monster.

I let out a sigh of relief when I stepped onto the basement floor. I tossed the three balls behind the furnace. And Burrrph rumbled after them.

Charlene stood halfway down the stairs. "He's used to being with a basement furnace," she said. "He'll be okay for the night."

I wished I could believe her. But I knew she was forcing herself to be cheerful.

We spun around and raced up the stairs. I closed the basement door carefully behind me.

Before we took two steps, Mom and Dad were in the hallway. A narrow miss!

"We're going to make you a snack—big stacks of pancakes," Dad said. "I'm surprised they didn't give you dinner at school."

"Everyone was too busy," I said. I turned to Charlene. "We were *very* busy, weren't we?"

She nodded. "Very busy."

We followed Mom and Dad into the kitchen. I kept glancing back, making sure the basement door stayed closed.

Mom pulled some eggs and butter from the fridge. Dad brought the big pancake skillet down from the cabinet and lowered it to the stove.

Mom searched the cabinets. Then she said something to Dad. I couldn't hear what she said. But Dad nodded and started to walk down the hall.

"Dad—where are you going?" I called after him.

"To the basement," he answered. "The pancake mix is in the downstairs pantry."

"NO!" I cried. "Let ME go! I'LL go!"

I started after him. Too late. He already had the basement door open. I heard his footsteps on the stairs.

Oh no. Oh no. Oh no.

A few seconds later, I heard his startled shout from the basement: "Hey! I don't believe it! What on earth IS this?"

41

"I can explain!" I screamed.

I flew down the basement stairs, taking them two at a time. I hit the basement floor so hard, I nearly fell on my face. "Dad . . . I—"

He stood at the pantry. One hand on the open pantry door. He turned to me. "Kelly—who did this? Who left the pantry door open?"

"Huh?" I gasped. My heart was in my throat. I started to choke.

"Someone left the pantry door open," Dad said. "You know we can't do that. Mice will get into our food."

"I . . . uh . . . well . . ." I gazed all around. Burrrph was nowhere to be seen. I realized he must be curled up behind the furnace.

"I . . . I don't think it was me," I stammered, finally finding my voice. "I always close the door."

Dad frowned at me. "I'll have to speak to your mother," he said. "We have to be careful to keep the door closed. All kinds of wildlife get into the basement."

"Yes. All kinds," I murmured.

I heard Burrrph grunt from behind the furnace.

Dad squinted at me. He thought it was me.

I followed him back upstairs. I closed the basement door carefully behind me.

A few minutes later, our late-night snack was served. Pancakes never tasted so good!

I could tell you what a lonnnng day Charlene and I had the next day. Of course, we thought Burrrph would come bursting out of the basement at any minute.

There was no school because of the party that night. It would have been nice to show Charlene around my new town. But we were afraid to leave the house.

After dinner, Mom and Dad both hugged me and wished me good luck. "You're the monster's date," Dad said. "Make us proud!"

"I'll try to stay alive," I told them.

"I like your attitude," Mom said. They disappeared out the front door. They were going to visit friends across town.

As soon as we heard their car back down the driveway, we rescued Burrrph from the basement. He seemed eager to leave. He followed my juggling up the stairs and out the house.

We kept in shadow as we made our way to my school. I took some shortcuts through backyards. We stayed far away from the streets, where we could be easily seen.

Juggling all the way, I brought Burrrph to the back door of the school. Lights poured out of the gym windows. I could hear voices and music from inside. A lot of kids were already at the party.

"I think everyone will be a little surprised," Charlene said.

"A little." I laughed.

Juggling faster, I guided the big monster into the school building. Then Charlene and I led him down the empty hall to the gym.

We paused outside the gym doors. "Friiight Night, here we come!" I exclaimed.

We pushed open the doors and led Burrrph into the gym.

42

Balloons bounced along the high ceiling. Streamers in all colors hung from the rafters. A wide mural covered one gym wall. Painted by Adams students, it showed Skwerm with his fists raised above his head, mouth open, raging at the sky.

Juggling hard, I led Burrrph onto the gym floor—and the screams began.

Screams of surprise. A lot of kids recognized Burrrph. They came running over, everyone shouting at once:

"What is he doing here?"

"How did you get him here?"

"I don't believe Burrrph is here!"

I walked backward to the middle of the gym, juggling rapidly, moving Burrrph across the glowing wood floor. He clumped loudly, his whole stingray-like body pulsing as if he were underwater. His black eyes gazed from side to side, watching the excited kids.

Charlene cupped her hands around her mouth and shouted at the top of her lungs. "Where is Skwerm? Bring Skwerm up to meet his date!"

And then Ms. Waxman came trotting across the gym. "Kelly—" she cried. "You've got Burrrph! You are the one who kidnapped Burrrph?"

I kept juggling. "Guilty," I said.

"I used to teach at Madison," she said. "So Burrrph and I are old friends." She gave Burrrph a short wave. "How did you do this, Kelly?" she demanded.

I sighed. "It wasn't easy."

She slapped me a high five. It almost made me drop the juggling balls. "Brilliant!" she exclaimed. "This is brilliant! Kelly, how *bold* of you!"

"Yes. Bold. It's my new personality," I said.

That made Charlene laugh.

"You kidnapped Burrrph," Ms. Waxman said. "So bold," she repeated. Her grin grew wider. "You ruined Madison Academy's Friiight Night—and you made our Friiight Night awesomely awesome!"

"That was the plan," I said. "Burrrph will be Skwerm's date. They'll hang together, and we kids will all be safe."

"Brilliant!" the teacher cried again. "This will be the best Friiight Night in history."

She motioned to some kids against the wall. "Hurry. Go get Skwerm," she ordered them. "Let's get this party started. Let's introduce Skwerm to his surprise date."

The teacher rubbed her hands together and grinned at Charlene and me. "This is going to be historic."

Of course, it didn't exactly go the way I had planned it.

43

While we waited for the kids to bring Skwerm up to the gym, Burrrph's flat fins began to wave as if he were swimming underwater. His black eyes gazed across the gym, staring at the kids who had gathered around.

What was he thinking?

What was he planning?

To attack?

No way.

Burrrph wouldn't want to attack if he had a friend to hang out with. *Would* he?

He began to make low grunting sounds. His body rippled, as if ocean waves were rushing through him. His round black eyes moved from kid to kid, then back to me.

Ms. Waxman's grin was frozen on her face as she watched him. She patted me on the back. "Good job, Kelly," she muttered.

I could see she was tense, too. We were all tense. All waiting to see what would happen when the two monsters met.

"Oh!" I jumped a mile when one of the helium balloons on the ceiling popped.

Kids screamed.

Burrrph didn't move. His fins continued to wave at his sides. I could picture him deep under the ocean swimming with other rays. Except that he was eight feet tall!

Waiting . . . Waiting . . .

What was taking the kids so long to bring Skwerm up?

Charlene had her hands dug deep in her jeans pockets. She kept bending her knees, like she was doing some kind of exercise.

I kept blowing out long whooshes of air. My eyes didn't leave the gym's double doors.

Waiting . . . Waiting . . .

Finally, the doors swung open.

I heard Skwerm before I saw him. Heard his groans and rough snarls, like an angry dog.

He didn't walk into the gym. He *poured* into the gym. Like an enormous blob with teeth and bulging eyes.

It seemed to take forever for the two monsters to see each other.

When their eyes locked, they both froze for a moment. Surprised. Then their mouths opened, and they both let loose with furious roars. Deafening, earsplitting roars.

I cried out and grabbed Charlene. I pulled her to safety as Skwerm roared right past her.

The two monsters ran at each other. When they

crashed together, the gym floor shook and the ceiling lights flickered.

Roaring furiously, they began to tear at each other. They attacked each other as we all gaped in shock and horror.

Slapping and tearing and biting. Their anger rushing out from deep inside them.

"What a disaster!" I cried, holding on to Charlene. "What was I *thinking*?!"

44

"No!" Charlene cried. She pushed me away. "Look, Kelly! You're wrong. Look at them!"

"Huh?" I stumbled away from her. I forced myself to take deep breaths. And I squinted hard at the two roaring monsters in the middle of the gym.

Wait. Whoa. Wait.

They weren't attacking each other. They were *hugging*.

They wrapped themselves around each other. And roaring to the ceiling, they did a fin-crushing, paw-slapping dance. The weirdest dance I ever saw.

But it was definitely dancing. Not fighting.

Kids began to step away from the far wall. We all formed a circle around the two enormous creatures to watch them dance and celebrate.

Ms. Waxman, still grinning, clapped me on the back again. "You're a hero, Kelly!" she exclaimed. "A total hero. This is the best Friiight Night in *history*!"

"Ms. Waxman," I said. "Can I get extra credit for this?"

* * *

The next morning, Charlene's mom came to pick her up and take her back to Little Hills Village. I helped her carry her bag to the car.

"I guess you won't be homesick anymore," Charlene said.

"Now that I'm a hero, I'm going to like it here," I said. "Especially since I have my bold new personality."

"You're not *that* great," she said. "You couldn't have done it without me."

"What exactly did you do?" I asked.

"I gave you moral support." She slammed the car door, and I watched them drive away.

I had to hurry to school. Ms. Waxman said she wanted to see me before class began.

Am I in trouble? I wondered.

Of course not. She probably wants to give me a reward!

She met me at the door to her classroom with a big smile on her face. "Good morning, Hero!" she gushed. "I'm so proud of you, Kelly. The whole school is proud of you."

I lowered my eyes modestly. "Thanks," I murmured.

"Come with me," she said. "I have a new assignment for you."

I followed her down the hall. "New assignment?"

She nodded. "Yes. I'm putting you in charge of Scaaary Saturday."

"Excuse me?" I said. "Scaaary Saturday? What's that?"

She turned to me. "That's our next party. Haven't you met the monster in the music room?"

EPILOGUE FROM SLAPPY

Hahaha. It's a good thing Kelly has a bold new personality. He's going to need it!

Skwerm is a pussycat compared to the monster in the music room.

That monster is a great musician. He turns kids into *accordions*! Hahaha! No music comes from the music room—only screams. And that's music to *my* ears!

Now, don't you worry. I'll be back soon with another *Goosebumps* story filled with screams for you.

Remember, this is *SlappyWorld*.

You only *scream* in it!

THE ONLY THING TO FEAR . . .
IS EVERYTHING.

TURN THE PAGE FOR A
SNEAK PEEK OF THE HOUSE OF
SHIVERS SERIES!

1

"PLEASE DON'T LEAVE US!"

Uncle Wendell loved to make up strange and frightening stories. So when he told my sister Betty and me about the scariest book ever written, we didn't believe him.

We knew he was trying to scare us. We were on to him. We only pretended to shiver and shudder.

Of course, we *should* have believed him about the Scariest Book Ever.

Because that story about the book was true.

The truth is, Betty and I didn't want to stay with Uncle Wendell. As we made the long drive to his house, even Bellamy was barking unhappily in the backseat beside us.

Bellamy is our five-year-old shepherd-terrier mix, and he's usually an angel in the car. But he knew something was up. He knew we were heading somewhere new and strange. So he didn't stop yapping.

We had been driving for hours. Trees whirred by in a green blur outside the car window. We were racing past some kind of forest.

"Mom, listen," I said. I leaned forward in my seat behind her and tapped her shoulder.

"Stop tapping me, Billy," she said. "You're like a woodpecker. You've been tapping me the whole drive."

"That's because I'm trying to get through to you," I said.

"You two have made your point," Dad growled, hunched over the steering wheel. "But you don't have a point. The only point is on the tops of your heads!"

Dad was a stand-up comic before he went into real estate. And he still thinks he's funny.

"We know you're anxious about staying with your uncle Wendell," Mom said.

"Anxious?" Betty cried. "We're not anxious. We don't want to stay with a total stranger for two weeks."

"Not so loud," Dad muttered.

"I can't help it. I was born with a loud voice," Betty replied. Betty is tough. She never lets Dad have the last word. And she never pretends to laugh at his jokes like I do.

My sister and I are twins. Billy and Betty, the Arnold twins. Dad always tells people we're identical twins. And that doesn't even begin to be funny. We don't even look alike. She's tall and thin and I'm at least four inches shorter.

Twins are supposed to be close to one another, and we get along okay. Of course, everything isn't perfect. Mom told Betty she was ten minutes older than me. So she thinks she's the boss. The big sister.

I don't know why Mom had to tell her that. If I was ten minutes older, I wouldn't make such a big deal about it.

I was still leaning over Mom. The car hit a bump in the road, and it sent me sailing back into my seat.

Dad laughed. "This is a thrill ride," he said, watching me in the rearview mirror.

I growled. "You know I hate roller coasters."

"Everybody, simmer down," Mom said.

"Billy and I are simmered *up*," Betty said. "You said Uncle Wendell is a weird one. I heard you saying that to Dad. "So why are we staying with him?"

"He was the only person who could take you both for two weeks," Mom said. "We have no other family. We've been over this, haven't we?"

"You two are *both* weird ones," Dad said, a grin on his face. "So you'll get along fine."

Betty rubbed Bellamy's belly, and he rolled onto his back and stopped yapping for a while. Betty is his favorite. When I rub his belly, he tries to bite me.

I had to sneeze. I tried to hold it in. But a loud blast escaped my nose and mouth.

"Billy, cover your nose," Dad said.

"There wasn't time," I told him. "You know I always sneeze when I'm tense or upset."

"Think you could try to outgrow that habit?" Dad asked.

"Why can't we go to London with you?" I demanded for the hundredth time.

Dad groaned. "I told you, Billy. It's a business trip. Not a family vacation."

"The two weeks will fly by," Mom said. She turned in her seat. "Can I just talk seriously to you for two minutes?"

"Okay. We'll grant you permission," Betty replied. Sometimes she acts like she's a queen or something.

"I know you have no memory of Wendell," Mom said. "He saw you when you were babies. But I think you're really going to like him. He—"

"You said he was weird," I said, "and his house sits all by itself in a forest with no one around for miles."

"You are going to *love* his old house," Dad chimed in. "And it isn't just *any* forest. It's called the Wayward Forest."

Betty rolled her eyes. "Huh? Wayward? Why do they call it that?"

"Beats me," Dad said. He swerved to miss a hole in the road.

"You didn't let me finish," Mom said, reaching for a water bottle. "You two like to read. You're both bookworms."

"Ugh," Betty groaned. "Why do we have to be worms?"

"Well, Wendell has an amazing collection of books," Mom said. "I think you will go nuts when you explore his library."

"Yeah. Nuts," I repeated sarcastically.

"And his house is filled with wild gadgets and strange objects he has collected from all over the world," Mom added. "The house is like a museum."

"Awesome. I always wanted to live in a museum," I muttered.

Dad slapped his hand on the steering wheel. "Bad attitude!" he shouted. "Both of you. Bad attitude! You should be open to new experiences."

"I don't want experiences," I said. "I just want to stay with someone I know."

"I'll bet when we come to pick you up in two weeks, you won't want to leave," Mom said.

It was my turn to roll my eyes. I wanted to say: *"How much do you want to bet?"*

But I didn't say it.

An hour later, Dad gripped the steering wheel tightly in both hands. He gritted his teeth. "I think we're totally lost. Mom and I are going to miss our flight," he said.

Mom patted his arm. "We'll be okay. I'm sure we're close to Wendell's house."

We had swung off the highway. The dirt roads through the forest twisted and curved through the trees, and Dad got turned around twice.

"We're making a circle," he said. "I remember that pile of rocks."

"Go straight. Go straight." Mom pointed out the windshield. "I think we're okay."

Dad shook his head. "I—I was counting on the navigation system to get us there."

The GPS had gone out as soon as we turned off the highway.

"Yaaay!" I cried. "Does this mean we get to go to London with you?"

"*Be quiet, Billy!*" Dad shouted. "You're not helpful at all."

I sank back in my seat. Betty stared out the window. "We can't be lost," she said. "People don't get lost anymore, do they?"

"No. We're not," Mom said. "Look! I think that's Wendell's house. I see it back in the trees."

Dad mopped the sweat off his forehead with one hand. "Whew. Lucky the house is so tall. Whoa. Look at it. Rising high above the treetops."

The car bumped into a small clearing. Dad turned into a long, pebbly driveway that led past a grassy front lawn up to the house.

Now I could see the house clearly. It wasn't shaped like a house. It rose straight up like a tower. A solid black tower. The afternoon sunlight didn't reflect off it. It made me think of blackboard slate.

I could see a narrow door. A row of tiny windows along the front of the house.

"Is it a house or a fort?" Betty asked.

Mom and Dad didn't answer. They were already standing in the driveway, pulling our suitcases from the trunk.

Bellamy scratched his paws against the window. It had been a long drive for the poor guy. I could see he was desperate to get out.

I grabbed his leash, pushed open the door, and slid my feet to the ground. Bellamy wagged his tail happily and tried to tug me toward the woods.

The sun hung low over the forest, and the air felt cool and fresh. Birds trilled and whooped, as if greeting us.

Dad checked the time on his phone. "Whoa. We are so late. We really have to hurry."

He carried our suitcases to the front door and dropped them. He pushed the brass doorbell.

Betty and I hung back, waiting for Uncle Wendell to appear. What did he look like? I had no memory of him.

With an impatient sigh, Dad pushed the doorbell again. Silence.

No Uncle Wendell.

Dad pounded his fist on the door.

"I'll bet he went into town to buy groceries," Mom said. "He asked for a list of all the food you two like."

Dad shook his head. "We can't wait here. We'll miss our flight." He mopped sweat off his forehead. "I'm so sorry, but we have to go. Everything will be fine. I'm sure Wendell will be back any minute."

He grabbed Mom's arm and started to pull her to the car.

"You're just going to leave us here?" I called after them.

"Apologize to Wendell for us," Mom said. "Tell him we didn't want to miss our plane."

She bent to pet the dog. "Take good care of Bellamy," she said. "And have fun. Text us as soon as Wendell arrives so we know you're okay."

They climbed into the car and closed the doors. We watched them back down the driveway and roar away, the pebbles flying from under the tires.

I opened my mouth in a loud sneeze. You can guess I was a little tense.

I wiped my nose with my sleeve and pushed the doorbell again.

No answer.

Suddenly, Bellamy began tugging us away from the door, pulling hard on his leash. The dog opened his jaws and began to howl.

Betty and I gazed up at the strange black house. The late afternoon sunlight glinted off its tiny windows.

Bellamy howled louder.

"What's wrong with him?" Betty asked. "Does he know something we don't know?"

"IS THIS THE WRONG HOUSE?"

"Bellamy, what's your problem?" I demanded. "Stop howling."

He dug his paws into the ground and refused to budge. Finally, Betty bent down and petted his back, soothing him.

"I think he picked up on our fear," I said. I'd read a thing online about how dogs can sense how their owners feel.

"I'm not afraid," Betty said, shaking her head. "I just don't want to do this. Where is Uncle Wendell? Is he home or not?"

I thought maybe Bellamy's howls would bring Wendell outside. But the door remained closed. Silence inside.

We both stared at the narrow black door. Bellamy had stopped howling. But his back was still tensed.

I pounded my fist on the door. It didn't make much of a sound. The door seemed very thick.

Betty shivered. The air had grown chilly in the shadow of the house. A breeze had started to pick up, and the trees all shook and whispered. A big brown rabbit stood on its hind legs and stared at us from the tall grass of the front lawn.

We gazed at each other, waiting for Wendell to open the door.

Waiting.

"Maybe Mom was right. Maybe he went out," I said. My voice trembled a little.

"But he's expecting us," Betty said, staring at the door. "He knows we're arriving this afternoon." She shivered again. Bellamy shivered, too.

I closed my fist and pounded again, as hard as I could.

A bird cawed loudly from somewhere behind us.

Now I shivered. Was it trying to warn us away?

I turned and walked to the tiny window nearest the door. Shielding my eyes with both hands, I peered into the house.

Total darkness.

"No lights on," I told Betty. "I can't see anything."

"He *has* to be in there," Betty said, rubbing Bellamy's back. She opened her mouth and began to shout. "Uncle Wendell? Wendell! We're out here. Can you hear us?"

Silence.

The brown rabbit turned and scampered into the trees.

"Wendell? Wendell? Are you there?" Betty tried again.

I stepped up to the door. I raised my fist to pound on it one more time. But then I had a better idea.

I wrapped my hand around the small brass door knob. I turned it and pushed. And the door creaked open.

Bellamy made a *yip* sound and tried to back away.

I pushed the door open farther. Betty grabbed Bellamy and pulled him inside with us.

It was almost as dark as night. We both stopped and waited for our eyes to adjust. The air felt cold and damp, and the room smelled musty, as if it hadn't been dusted in a very long time.

I rubbed my hand over the wall, and it bumped a light switch. A gray light washed down from the ceiling high above us.

Blinking, I peered around the room. It was a huge square room with a ceiling a mile high. I saw a long wooden table with two chairs behind it. And there were two overstuffed lounge chairs at the far end of the room.

Bellamy took off for one of the overstuffed chairs. "Come back!" Betty called. Her voice echoed off the walls. But the dog ignored her. He was too busy sniffing it.

I cupped my hands around my mouth. "Wendell!" I shouted. "Hey, Uncle Wendell. It's Billy and Betty. We're here!"

The words echoed into the distance.

I heard a *creak*. I thought maybe Wendell was finally coming. But no. It must have been old house noises.

"Wendell? Wendell?" Betty and I both called his name.

Still no answer.

I turned to my sister. "Didn't Mom say his house was filled with books and all kinds of crazy objects?"

She nodded.

"Well, look around," I said. "No books anywhere. The room is nearly bare. No weird objects and not a single book."

Betty wrinkled her forehead. She took a deep, shuddering breath. "Do you think maybe this is the wrong house?"

A TRAP

We called Wendell's name some more. Our voices echoed as if we were in a cave.

I spotted a door at the other end of the room. It was open. Nothing but darkness behind it.

"Wendell! Uncle Wendell? Are you here?"

We really didn't expect an answer, so we both jumped when a man came rumbling through the doorway.

He took four or five heavy steps, boots thudding loudly on the floor. Then he stopped and his eyes went wide when he saw us.

Startled, Betty and I froze. Bellamy barked once, then stood at attention.

He was a big man with a lion's mane of black hair, wild around his head, and a spiky black beard. He wore a loose-fitting, plaid lumberjack's shirt over baggy khaki pants and black knee-high boots.

He squinted at us, his big chest heaving up and

down, breathless, as if he didn't expect us. He rubbed his beard with a pudgy hand. "Hello there," he said finally. His voice was deep and scratchy.

"Uncle Wendell?" I said. "We—"

"You're here," he said. His black eyes studied us. They moved from Betty to me. He rubbed his beard some more, as if he was thinking hard.

"Our parents were late," Betty said. "They couldn't stay to see you. They are sorry, but—"

"You've grown," he said in his rumbly voice.

"Betty and I are twelve," I said.

He nodded. Then he took a few steps closer. "I want to apologize. I was out back. I wasn't here to greet you."

"That's okay," I said. "We—we're so glad—"

Wendell lowered his eyes. "I'm afraid you've come at a bad time."

"A bad time?"

What did he mean by *that*?

"But can we still stay here?" Betty asked.

"Yes. You *must* stay here," he said. "I need your help."

He waved a big hand, motioning for us to follow him.

Betty and I exchanged glances. *What is going on here? Why does he need our help?*

About the Author

R.L. Stine says he gets to scare people all over the world. So far, his books have sold more than 400 million copies, making him one of the most popular children's authors in history. The Goosebumps series has more than 150 titles and has inspired a TV series and two motion pictures. R.L. himself is a character in the movies! He has also written the teen series Fear Street, and the Mostly Ghostly and Nightmare Room series. He is currently writing a series of graphic novels entitled Just Beyond. R.L. Stine lives in New York City with his wife, Jane, an editor and publisher. You can learn more about him at rlstine.com.

Catch the MOST WANTED Goosebumps® villains UNDEAD OR ALIVE!

SPECIAL EDITIONS

THE SCARIEST PLACE ON EARTH!

Goosebumps HorrorLand
HELP! WE HAVE STRANGE POWERS!
R.L. STINE
SCHOLASTIC

Goosebumps HorrorLand
ESCAPE FROM HORRORLAND
R.L. STINE
SCHOLASTIC

Goosebumps HorrorLand
THE STREETS OF PANIC PARK
R.L. STINE
SCHOLASTIC

Goosebumps HorrorLand
WHEN THE GHOST DOG HOWLS
R.L. STINE
SCHOLASTIC

Goosebumps HorrorLand
LITTLE SHOP OF HAMSTERS
R.L. STINE
SCHOLASTIC

Goosebumps HorrorLand
HEADS, YOU LOSE!
R.L. STINE
SCHOLASTIC

Goosebumps HorrorLand
WEIRDO HALLOWEEN
R.L. STINE
SCHOLASTIC

Goosebumps HorrorLand
THE WIZARD OF OOZE
R.L. STINE
SCHOLASTIC

Goosebumps HorrorLand
SLAPPY NEW YEAR!
R.L. STINE
SCHOLASTIC

Goosebumps HorrorLand
THE HORROR AT CHILLER HOUSE
R.L. STINE
SCHOLASTIC

HALL OF HORRORS—HALL OF FAME FOR THE TRULY TERRIFYING!

Goosebumps HALL OF HORRORS
CLAWS!
R.L. STINE
SCHOLASTIC

Goosebumps HALL OF HORRORS
NIGHT OF THE GIANT EVERYTHING
R.L. STINE
SCHOLASTIC

The Original Bone-Chilling Series

R.L. Stine's Fright Fest!
Now with Splat Stats and More!

GET YOUR HANDS ON THEM BEFORE THEY GET THEIR HANDS ON YOU!

ALL 62 ORIGINAL **Goosebumps** AVAILABLE IN EBOOK!

SCHOLASTIC
scholastic.com

GBCLRP2

CONTINUE THE FRIGHT AT THE GOOSEBUMPS SITE
scholastic.com/goosebumps

FANS OF GOOSEBUMPS CAN:

- PLAY THE GHOULISH GAME:
  GOOSEBUMPS: SLAPPY'S DROP DEAD HOUSE

- LEARN ABOUT NEW BOOKS AND TERRIFYING CLASSICS

- TAKE A QUIZ AND LEARN WHICH TYPE OF MONSTER YOU ARE!

- LEARN ABOUT THE AUTHOR WHO STARTED IT ALL: R.L. STINE

SCHOLASTIC

GBWEB2019

GOOSEBUMPS
SLAPPYWORLD

THIS IS SLAPPY'S WORLD— YOU ONLY SCREAM IN IT!